Revenge

Also in this series:
Hard Boiled Love: An Anthology of Noir Love
Iced: The New Noir Anthology of Cold, Hard Fiction

Revenge

A noir anthology about getting even

Edited by Kerry J. Schooley and Peter Sellers

INSOMNIAC PRESS

Copyright © 2004 by by Kerry J. Schooley and Peter Sellers

All rights reserved. No part of this publication may be reproduced, stored in a retrieval system or transmitted, in any form or by any means, without the prior written permission of the publisher or, in case of photocopying or other reprographic copying, a license from Access Copyright, 1 Yonge Street, Suite 1900, Toronto, Ontario, Canada, M5E 1E5.

Copy edited by Emily Schultz
Interior designed by Marijke Friesen

Library and Archives Canada Cataloguing in Publication

Revenge : a noir anthology about getting even / edited by Kerry Schooley and Peter Sellers.

ISBN 1-894663-68-3

1. Short stories, Canadian (English) 2. Canadian fiction (English)—21st century. 3. Revenge—Fiction. I. Schooley, Kerry J., 1949-
II. Sellers, Peter, 1956-

PS8323.H67R49 2004   C813'.0108353   C2004-903952-0

The publisher gratefully acknowledges the support of the Canada Council, the Ontario Arts Council and the Department of Canadian Heritage through the Book Publishing Industry Development Program.

Printed and bound in Canada

Insomniac Press
192 Spadina Avenue, Suite 403
Toronto, Ontario, Canada, M5T 2C2
www.insomniacpress.com

Table of Contents

Introduction, *Kerry J. Schooley and Peter Sellers*	7
A Wanton Disregard, *Jean Rae Baxter*	9
A Murder Coming, *James Powell*	31
Bush Fever, *Peter Sellers*	39
An Eye for an Eye, *Nancy Kilpatrick*	47
Italics, *Fabrizio Napoleone*	53
Green Ghetto, *Vern Smith*	65
Great Minds, *Barbara Fradkin*	87
The Big Trip, *John Swan*	99
Dead Like Dogs, *William Bankier*	113
Crocodile Tears, *Leslie Watts*	129
Hunky, *Hugh Garner*	141
Man on the Roof, *Jas. R. Petrin*	155

Introduction

If you prick us, do we not bleed? If you tickle us, do we not laugh? If you poison us, do we not die? And if you wrong us, shall we not revenge?
—William Shakespeare, *The Merchant of Venice*, II, ix. 66

Ah revenge. Vengeance. Retaliation. A pound of flesh. Blood for blood. Tooth for tooth. An eye for an eye. The day of reckoning. The settling of accounts. Keeping the wound green. Yes, there was a time when revenge was among the more reliable of human motivations.

How things have changed.

Today, with bullies in retreat like goons suspended from a hockey game, with family values rampant and justice a DNA-swab away, there are few occasions to experience the real slights that once fed primitive desires for revenge.

That is why we are so proud of this third collection of noir fiction, requiring as it does the skill to conjure unfamiliar forms of thought. Can you imagine, these days, feeling cheated by a business associate, or betrayed by a loved one? Can you imagine anyone, anymore, having cause for dissatisfaction with their criminal sentence? Can you imagine in our enlightened time, people scaling walls, donning disguises, travelling great distances, staging accidents, all to get even for some long-held grudge?

Relax gentle reader, it is not required that you do. The twelve authors who follow have already imagined these heresies for you. Your part is to surmise, with little more than a plot to go by, what sort of person might do such things, in the unlikely event that you should meet one in real life.

Here's a little limber-up: It is said that Pierre Trudeau, the olden-times Canadian prime minister famous for, among many things, heralding The Just Society, was once criticized for accepting private donations to install a swimming pool at the official residence on Sussex Drive.

"You may come over at any time to practice your diving," he told a particularly irritating opponent. "Even before the water is in."*

Strange times, eh?

---

*Fadiman, Clifton (ed.), *The Little, Brown Book of Anecdotes* (1985) pg. 552.

A Wanton Disregard
by Jean Rae Baxter

Jean Rae Baxter is a literary Jekyll and Hyde. An outwardly genteel, retired high school English teacher, Jean writes stories for children and young adults. But she also produces noir fiction of a particularly cunning and nasty bent. She demonstrated her dark side memorably in the story "Loss," which appeared in *Hard Boiled Love*, published in 2003 by Insomniac Press. Jean's work has been published in numerous literary journals and anthologies, winning awards from the *Canadian Writer's Journal* and the Hamilton and Region Arts Council. Her first collection of short stories is forthcoming from Seraphim Books in 2005.

Bill's cellphone rang. Damn! Vera again. Every two minutes for the last twenty! So what the hell was he supposed to do? He was already ten klicks over the limit, racing down Wyandotte.

He wouldn't answer, that's what. But the phone kept on ringing, and he answered it. He always did.

"Vera, can't you keep him happy for twenty minutes?"

"Mr. Sugarman's already been waiting twenty minutes. He was on time. You aren't."

"Make him a coffee."

"I've done that."

"Tell him it isn't my fault. I got held up at my last meeting. The client was late."

"He says if you're not here in ten minutes, his business goes elsewhere."

"Oh shit!" Bill swerved the car around a jaywalker. "Vera, you still there?"

"Yeah."

"Tell him ten minutes." Ten minutes to get back or a million dollar contract goes down the sewer.

Bill floored the accelerator.

That's when he felt the bump. Felt it. Saw nothing, until, all at once, a man's face looked in through the windshield. Eyes wide, staring into his. Mouth open. A hand waving. No, it was clutching air. Bill braked as the man rolled off the hood.

Screams on all sides. A woman shrieked, "The little boy's under the car!"

Bill opened the car door and swung his legs around to get out. His knees buckled, and he had to hang on to the doorframe to steady himself. All the air had been sucked out of his lungs.

When he looked down, he saw a small white sneaker, a blue sock, a plump leg that twitched and then lay still. Shiny drops of blood, bright as paint, lay splattered on the asphalt.

Twenty feet away, the man who had stared at Bill through the windshield lay motionless on the pavement, his eyes still wide open.

Bill sat down heavily on the car seat. He lowered his face into his hands. "What have I done?" he groaned. "What have I done?"

The framed picture that Lydia Carey kept on her bedside table was the first thing she saw every morning and the last thing she saw at night. It was there to help her remember the faces of her husband and child, and also to remind her that the price for their deaths had not been paid.

Lydia had taken the photograph in the backyard, a week before they died. Matthew and Mattie: father and son. Mattie is sitting on Matthew's shoulders. His hands rest on either side of his daddy's throat, plump little fingers spread wide. He is looking down into Matthew's face. Matthew, his head half turned, is looking up at his son. Their smiles are of perfect trust and love. Matthew is holding on to Mattie's legs just above his ankles. On the boy's feet are new white sneakers and blue socks.

Lydia had been in Mattie's room making the bed when two officers, a man and a woman, brought the news. The policewoman was black. She held tight to Lydia's hands. Lydia remembered her compassionate eyes, her warm West Indian voice and the strength that flowed from her hands.

The next door neighbour came over. She made tea, phoned relatives and stayed until the living room began to fill with people. Lydia's sister Diane was there. So were Lydia's mom and dad, and Matthew's parents and his two brothers. People lined the walls, sitting on the sofa, in the armchairs, on chairs brought in from the dining room and kitchen. The only clear space was the corner to the right of the fireplace where Lydia sat, her hands clutched on her lap, holding a sodden handkerchief. Her eyes were hot; her head pounded; everything was a blur. Somebody gave her a pill. Diane told her to go upstairs and lie down.

For no special reason, she went into Mattie's room, and found there a deep calm, despite the sound of voices from downstairs. She lay down on the half-made bed and hugged Mattie's pillow. His sheets smelled sweetly of soap and milk, mingled with a whiff of urine from the plastic mattress cover.

Stick-on stars twinkled on Mattie's bedroom ceiling. Ponies pranced, bears danced and circus clowns juggled on the walls. The floor was a jumble of toys. Silent drum. Oversized Lego for tiny fingers. A teddy bear, flat on its back, stared up at the starry sky.

Voices floated up. Frequently someone spoke her name, but she didn't care. After a while she got off the bed and sat on the floor amidst the toys. She picked up the teddy bear and held it on her lap while her mind struggled with vague and peculiar thoughts. She imagined that Mattie was hiding in the closet, and she squeezed her eyes shut.

"One, two three. Ready or not! Here I come." She listened for his little boy giggle.

"Mattie! Where are you?"

The day after the funeral, everyone left except Diane.

"You don't have to stay," said Lydia. "I'm fine."

"Sure you are. But my kids are at school all day. Joe can look after things for a couple of weeks. So don't argue."

Argue with Diane? What would be the point? As far back as Lydia could remember, Diane always won. And so she took over, filling the house with her bulky presence and with the sweet, comfortable smell of muffins and fresh-baked bread. Diane forced Lydia to eat. She watered plants, vacuumed, answered the phone. For the first few days she didn't talk too much; Lydia was grateful for that.

It was okay having her around as long as she didn't mind sleeping on the living room sofa. But after a week she started complaining that her back hurt. She needed a bed.

When Lydia didn't get the hint, she came right out and asked, "Will it be all right if I sleep in Mattie's room?"

Lydia pretended not to hear.

"Well, how about it?"

"Mattie's room?" Lydia started to sweat. "I don't think so."

"Why not?"

"Mattie's room should stay the way it is."

Diane put her arm around Lydia. "Honey, you can't make his room into a shrine. Denial makes things worse. You have to let go."

Lydia straightened her shoulders, took a deep breath, and held her body stiff against Diane's encircling arm. Denial was her only defence. How could she let it go?

"Listen to me," Diane said. "Grieving is a process. First there's shock. Then denial. That's where you are now. These are normal stages you have to go through in order to reach acceptance. You can't let yourself get stuck along the way."

"I don't believe it." Lydia spoke fiercely, for the thought of acceptance repelled her.

But Diane's insistent voice bombarded her with logic. Through habit and fatigue, Lydia caved in.

"I guess you're right," Lydia said.

"Of course I am." Diane gave Lydia's shoulder a squeeze and let her go. "Take Mattie's room. I'll change the sheets and pick up his toys."

"I can do that."

"No, I want to."

Lydia stripped off Mattie's sheets, took off the mattress cover and made up the bed. She returned the toys to the toy box and the teddy bear to its place on the shelf. When she had finished, the room did look more welcoming. And it was still Mattie's room, his to claim as soon as Diane left.

That evening Lydia helped Diane cook dinner. Afterward they made popcorn and watched TV the way they used to do when they were kids. Every minute, Lydia felt Diane's critical, appraising eyes upon her. All things considered, Lydia put on a good act.

"I'm going to be fine," she said as she clicked off the remote after the late news. "I can cope."

"I'll stay a few more days." Diane picked up the empty popcorn bowls to take them to the kitchen. "One thing we have to do is get some cartons from the supermarket so we can pack Matthew's clothes."

"What for?" Lydia's stomach clenched.

"To take to the Salvation Army."

"Not Matthew's clothes." She turned swiftly toward her sister, feeling the blood rise to her face. On this she would not yield.

"Sorry," said Diane. "I didn't mean to upset you. You're bound to feel anger. I guess you're reaching that stage."

Lydia felt hostile, yet spoke gravely, as if to a stranger. "You know I don't believe that stuff. It's too mechanical, as if people were robots."

"Yeah, well, it does happen."

"Not for me."

The next day, at dinner time, Joe phoned. He and the boys needed Diane. They had run out of clean underwear and the house was a mess.

"You'd think a grown man could manage a house and a couple of kids for a few weeks," she said with a touch of smugness.

"They miss you. Go home and take care of them."

"I guess I should." Diane shifted uncomfortably, as if she had something awkward to say. "If you don't mind me asking, are you okay for money?"

Lydia did mind, but answered calmly, "More than okay."

"Are you sure? Because if you need ...."

"Don't worry. Matthew had mortgage insurance and life insurance. Two hundred thousand." She paused. "Double for accidental death."

Diane's eyes widened. "That's a good bit of money."

"It takes off the pressure."

Lydia stood up abruptly to show that the subject was closed and put on the kettle for tea. "Now I have a question for you."

"Sure."

"Tell me about the man who drove the car."

When Diane didn't answer, Lydia turned around to face her. Diane was staring at some invisible spot on the wall. "You mustn't think about him. It interferes with..."

Lydia interrupted. "I don't want to hear about the grieving process. Just tell me about the man who drove the car. I have a right to know."

"Dwelling on it won't help you in the slightest."

"Tell me."

"I just know what was in the newspaper."

"I wasn't reading the newspapers."

Diane turned her eyes toward Lydia. "His name is William Shaw, known as Bill, and he's a sales rep for a developer."

"I want personal stuff."

"He's thirty-six. Married. Coaches kids' hockey."

"So he has children." Lydia kept her voice casual as she lifted the teapot from its shelf.

"I guess so."

"Boys? Girls? How old?"

"I'm not sure."

"Don't tell me you don't know."

"Okay." Diane sighed. "He has a ten-year-old girl who plays hockey for the Riverbank Mosquitoes. And another girl in kindergarten."

"Thanks." That was what Lydia needed to know.

During breakfast they reminisced about family vacations and childhood pets. Lydia kept up a stream of small talk, avoiding any topic that might cause Diane to lengthen her stay.

"Joe and the kids will be happy to get you back," she said as she started to clear the table.

"Yeah. Clean underwear and real food. Even kids get tired of pizza."

"You better get packed if you want to be home in time to cook supper."

Diane glanced at the kitchen wall clock. Nine-thirty. She stood up, carrying her coffee. "You're right. I should be on the road by ten."

Lydia listened to Diane's footsteps overhead. Ten more minutes. Five more minutes. The toilet flushed. One more minute.

At ten on the button, Diane came downstairs. Lydia walked her out to the car and waved good-bye. When Diane's car had disappeared around the corner, Lydia went inside. She closed the front door and leaned against it, listening to the silence.

After a few minutes, a car approached. It stopped outside, and the car door slammed. Christ! Had Diane come back? Lydia held her breath until silence returned, then tiptoed up the stairs to the bedroom that had been hers and Matthew's.

Matthew had his own closet off the master bedroom, and Lydia had hers. That was a feature Lydia loved about this house: two big walk-in closets. Since Matthew's death, she had avoided entering his. Once or twice she had gone in to hang something up, but left in haste.

Now, as she stood in front of the closed closet door, a feeling came over her that Matthew was very near. Not his spirit. This was physical. As her right hand turned the doorknob, her left strayed toward the light switch, then drew back. She slipped inside and shut the door behind her.

In the darkness and warmth, she inhaled the smell of Matthew: his sweat, his aftershave. She hugged his clothes, rubbed her cheeks against the rough tweed of his jacket, ran her hands up and down his jeans. Burrowing into the fleece of his sheepskin coat, she almost felt his body touching hers.

Then the telephone rang, and the illusion was gone. Lydia raised her head. Maybe Diane was calling from out on the highway. Flat tire. Breakdown. Accident. Yes, she must answer the phone.

Light rushed in as Lydia opened the closet door. She stumbled around to the far side of the bed, where the phone sat on Matthew's bedside table.

"Hello?"

A woman's voice, but not Diane's. Lydia recognized the West Indian tones.

"Good morning, Mrs. Carey. I'm Staff Sergeant Wallace at the Central Police Station. Constable Burns and I..."

"Yes. I remember you."

"I'm calling to tell you that I'm assigned as your contact person."

"Contact person?"

"I'm the officer who'll keep in touch with you through the court process."

"You mean through the trial?"

"There'll be no trial. Mr. Shaw is pleading guilty. With twenty witnesses watching him run the red light, plus his own statement after the accident, he thought he might as well get the whole thing over. The only question that remains is the sentence."

"How long will he be in jail?"

"That's up to the judge. All sorts of factors affect sentencing."

"In a case like this, what would be normal?"

"For Criminal Negligence Causing Death, maybe one year."

Lydia sat in Number One Courtroom beside Diane, who had returned to lend sisterly support. Bill Shaw, behind Plexiglas in the prisoner's box, wore a dark grey suit, blue shirt, and striped maroon and grey tie. Shouldn't he be wearing drab prison clothes? It was all wrong for him to look well-dressed, his sandy hair neatly combed.

He sat with his arms folded across his chest, as if he were trying to hold in his feelings. Once or twice his eyes scanned the watching public, but most of the time he was looking at his wife, an olive-skinned woman with darkly arched brows and a long nose, who constantly dabbed her eyes with a tissue. She wore a blue maternity dress with a pleated front.

"Did you know she was pregnant?" Diane whispered.

"No."

"Looks about seven months."

"Six or seven."

"I feel sorry for her."

"I don't."

"It would be horrible to give birth while your husband was in jail."

"I couldn't care less."

Lydia read her victim impact statement to the court. As she read, she had the feeling that the statement was about someone else, though every word was true. She had lost her husband's love and companionship. She had lost the joy of caring for her child and of watching him grow to manhood. Her desolation at having both husband and child snatched from her was complete and irremediable.

As she finished, Lydia stared straight at Bill Shaw. His face had turned pale, and when her eyes met his, he turned his head away.

When Lydia returned to her seat, she saw that Mrs. Shaw had given up dabbing her eyes with her tissue. Sobbing noisily, she let the tears roll down her cheeks. Pregnancy does that, Lydia thought, makes women broody and tender-hearted.

Suddenly Mrs. Shaw stopped sobbing. A look of wonder crossed her face as she placed her hand on her abdomen. Lydia understood. She remembered the feeling, that soft pummelling from inside, the bumping of a tiny knee or shoulder. It wasn't fair! Why should Bill Shaw's wife have this baby, and she no child at all?

Diane grabbed her arm. "Get a grip," she whispered.

"What?"

"You're crying."

Lydia blew her nose and sat up stiffly.

The defense attorney described his client's contrition. How those six seconds had changed his life. How he would never forgive himself.

The judge appeared unmoved. "Individual deterrence is not the only issue," he said, looking at his notes. "I don't expect this particular offender to appear in court again on a similar charge. But the public has to get the message. Conduct that shows a wanton disregard for the lives or safety of other persons must be criminally punished. He was driving fifteen kilometres over the speed limit while talking on his cellphone. He ran a red light and killed two people."

Bill Shaw got fourteen months imprisonment and a three-year driving suspension.

His lawyer asked the court to recommend admission to the temporary absence program so that the convicted man could continue his employment, for he was married with two young children and a third on the way.

The judge shook his head. "General deterrence must be considered in a case like this. A custodial sentence is required."

Back at the house, Lydia threw her coat on the sofa and went straight for the liquor cabinet. She pulled out a bottle of Scotch. "I need this."

"When did you start drinking?"

"Today. Right now."

"Put the bottle away," Diane said. "I'll make a pot of tea and we can talk."

"What's there to talk about? Shaw got fourteen months." She poured herself a drink and gulped it down.

"You think it should be more?"

"Fourteen years," she said viciously.

"Well, that's not going to happen."

"That's the problem." Lydia poured another drink. She waved the bottle at Diane. "Sure you won't have one?"

Diane shook her head.

"Don't look so glum," said Lydia. "Help is on the way." She downed her drink and reached for the bottle again.

"What help?"

"I dunno. Something."

Diane pursed her lips. "The help you need isn't in that bottle. Get some therapy. Join a support group. You could even go to church."

Lydia laughed. "You're not the first person to suggest that. Remember the minister who did the funeral? He paid a pastoral call to see how I was getting on." She mimicked a preachy voice, "'We must forgive those who sin against us.' I told him where he could stick that."

"Don't talk like that," said Diane. "It isn't healthy."

That night Lydia could not sleep. The photograph of Matthew and Mattie was the last thing she looked at before turning out the light. But when she closed her eyes, the face she saw was that of Mrs. Shaw, tears dribbling down her cheeks. She too must be sleepless tonight. But her loss wouldn't last forever. In a few months, her man would return to her bed. Even now she was not truly alone. In other bedrooms were her other children, and in her womb the one yet to be born.

Would it be a boy or a girl? After two girls, she probably wanted a boy. Or did she care? Would her child be dark like her or fair like Shaw?

Mattie had been like his father. They'd had the same brown eyes and curly hair. Matthew's was black. Mattie's was blond, but would have darkened as he matured.

Lydia turned on the bedside light. Yes, there they were: Mattie on Matthew's shoulders, looking down into his father's face. For the first time she noticed that their radiant smiles were only for each other. Her husband and her son had shut her out. A cold feeling came over her. Would they ever smile for her again?

Drifting into sleep, she heard a baby cry. With desperate urgency she followed the sound through dark and endless corridors. The crying grew louder. The baby waited for her, fled, then waited again. She was getting close. It was right around the next corner. But as soon as she turned the corner, it had moved on. Yet with every step she gained upon it. One more corner and she would have it. She turned the corner, and there was Mattie reaching out to her. She bent to hug him but woke as his arms tightened around her neck.

Lydia sat up and turned on the light. In the framed photograph on her bedside table, Matthew and Mattie smiled.

Outside the window, darkness had paled to the greyish light of early dawn. Too early to rise, too late to get to sleep again. But she had to do something, not just lie there. Lydia swung her legs over the side of the bed. On bare feet she crossed the floor to Matthew's closet.

His clothes—jackets, pants, coats—all hung on the rack just as before. But now they smelled stale, musty and slightly unclean. Strange how completely they had lost the power to stir her. Maybe Diane was right. Maybe this was progress to a further stage. Shock, denial, anger—she'd had them all. But Diane was wrong about acceptance. Lydia saw it now with perfect clarity: the final stage had to be revenge.

One by one, she lifted Matthew's clothes from the rack and stacked them on the bedroom floor. Later, Diane would help to pack them up for the Salvation Army; she'd be delighted to see her sister moving forward.

Emptied of clothes, Matthew's closet seemed spacious. Lydia had forgotten how large it was: four feet by eight. How did that compare with a jail cell? She could keep a captive here. A small captive. A thrill ran through her veins to think of it. An eye for an eye. A tooth for a tooth. A child for a child.

For one crazy minute, she thought it might work. Mattie's baby furniture—crib, changing table, chest of drawers—would fit in here. Diapers, sheets and blankets could go on the closet shelf. The police might search, but they'd find nothing. All she had to do was move the IKEA bookcase from Matthew's study and erect it here to cover the doorframe. They wouldn't suspect a second closet in her bedroom.

Yeah, but every time the baby needed a bottle or a diaper change, she'd have to unshelve all the books and move a seven-foot bookcase. And what if the baby cried at the wrong time, like during a police search or when people dropped in? Duct tape? No. This wouldn't work.

But the basic idea was brilliant. Kid snatching happened all the time—non-custodial parents abducting their child. They never got caught. Every month a different notice appeared on the back of her Visa bill envelope: MISSING/DISPARU, case number, date of birth, missing since... A picture taken before the abduction, then a projection of what the child would look like two, five years, ten years later.

For perfect justice, Bill Shaw's child should never be returned. But this was not a perfect world. How long, then? Not ten years, or five, or even two. Too expensive. Too much restriction on her own life. How about six months? Yes. Half a year of sitting in a prison cell not knowing where his child was, whether dead or alive, suffering, starving, or in pain.

Afterward, she could leave the baby in a basket on the Children's Aid Society steps, or in the women's washroom at the mall. Justice tempered with mercy had a pleasing sound.

With a bunch of flowers in her hand, Lydia roamed the halls of Grace Hospital, checking details like the right kind of ID badge to buy. She noted schedules and mentally charted the best route from the maternity ward to stairways, elevators, washrooms, exits. Fortunately, one hospital handled all the city's maternity cases. Barring some unusual circumstance, this was where Mrs. Shaw would give birth to the killer's child.

There were plenty of ads in the newspaper. "Reliable, responsible woman will give loving care." That's not the woman Lydia needed. "Responsible, reliable" would want an OHIP number. She'd ask questions, and if she didn't like the answers, she'd phone Children's Aid or even the police.

Nor could Lydia place her own ad. "Abductor seeks babysitter for kidnapped newborn." Well, of course she wouldn't say that! But a paid advertisement leaves a trail, and the trail would lead to her.

The ideal caregiver would ask no questions. She'd be someone desperate, marginalized, and not very smart. Downtown were shelters, shop doorways, underpasses, and the mean streets where panhandlers disappeared after the theatre crowd went home. Lydia's search would begin there.

It was snowing, and a couple of inches were already on the ground when Lydia emerged from the underground parking lot onto Wellington Square. Christmas lights twinkled amidst the branches of sidewalk trees and evergreen wreaths hung from lampposts.

Lydia had filled one coat pocket with loonies so she wouldn't have to fish for change in her handbag every time she saw a woman who might do. But for an hour she walked around Wellington Square and up and down Albert Street without success. Where were all the women beggars when she needed one? Lydia's boots leaked and she needed to pee. Maybe it was time to stop for lunch. After a Big Mac and a washroom break, she'd try the business district. Lydia's fingers closed on the loonies in her pocket.

Then, across the street, Lydia saw a girl huddled near the doorway of the Rendezvous Bar with a gym bag on the sidewalk beside her, mutely lifting her cupped hands to passers-by. For the five minutes that Lydia watched, no one dropped a coin. Most passers-by seemed not to see her. Everything about her said "beaten dog." Lydia crossed the street.

Close up, the girl looked like a child decked out for Hallowe'en. Black lips, black-lined eyes, white cheeks. Vampire maiden. So many hoops pierced the outer edge of her right ear that it looked like the spiral-coil spine of a pocket notebook.

Lydia dropped a loonie into her upraised hands. Then another loonie. The girl's green eyes widened. She knew something was up.

"I'm going to have lunch," Lydia said. "Will you join me?"

"Give me a couple more loonies and I'll buy my own."

"No. I want to talk to you."

"You a social worker?" The girls' eyes narrowed.

"Nothing like that. It's just ... well, I might have a job that would interest you."

"What kinda job?"

"Taking care of a baby."

"You're looking for a babysitter?"

"Come have lunch at McDonald's. We can talk about it if you're interested."

She screwed up one eye. "I might be."

The girl picked up her gym bag. Standing, she looked smaller and thinner than sitting down. Five-foot-one, ninety pounds was Lydia's guess. About fifteen. Homeless, probably. A girl of the shelters and the streets.

Maybe a hooker. But who would pay for that meagre body?

They walked without speaking, side by side through snow that was quickly changing to slush. When they got to McDonald's, the girl paused just inside the entrance while her eyes darted around piercingly, like a animal's looking out through a thicket.

"You're hungry?" Lydia asked.

She nodded.

Lydia bought her a Big Mac, a soft drink, fries, and an apple turnover. The girl devoured the food. Lydia ate a Big Mac, drank a coffee, then went to the washroom. When she returned, the girl had finished.

"What's your name?" she asked.

"Fiona."

"Fiona what?"

"Just Fiona."

A runaway. That was fine. First names were fine. "I'm Lenore," said Lydia. "Just Lenore."

"How old is your baby?"

"Not my baby. I'm helping a friend who's due any day. When her baby is born, she can't take it home or her father will kill her."

"Why doesn't she get it adopted?"

"She wants to keep it. But for now it has to be secret. Next summer, her boyfriend will come for her, and she'll be able to take the baby back."

Fiona looked as if this were perfectly reasonable. "So she needs a babysitter until next summer. Where's the kid going to stay if she can't take it home?"

"Your place."

"You got to be kidding. I don't have a place."

"If you take the job, I'll get you an apartment for six months. I'll supply everything and pay you fifty dollars a day. Cash. But you must be discreet."

"Meaning what?"

"You have to pretend it's your baby."

"Why?"

"No questions. I'm sworn to secrecy. If you have a problem with that, better tell me now."

"No problem."

"Fine. So this is what you have to do: be at the same spot outside the Rendezvous every day between eleven and one o'clock. Twenty bucks a day just to be there. I'll be checking. When the job starts, that's where I'll pick you up."

Mrs. Nagbor's white hair was tied back in a bun. Her cheeks were wrinkled and yellow and most of the colour had faded from the pupils of her eyes. She spoke very little English, barely enough to communicate that Mr. Nagbor, recently deceased, had always looked after finding tenants for the basement apartment in their house. Sitting in Mrs. Nagbor's cramped living room, Lydia nodded understandingly. She would be happy to pay seven hundred dollars per month, first and last in advance. Cash would be fine. And no lease.

The apartment came furnished. Mrs. Nagbor even owned a crib, which she would set up. She had no objection to a single mother with a baby, so long as the rent got paid.

Lydia purchased formula, bottles, diapers, wipes and creams in drugstores where she was not known. Everything went straight to Mrs. Nagbor's basement apartment. The devil was in the details, Lydia reminded herself. If she tripped up, something tiny would be the cause, like a receipt forgotten in a drawer.

She bought a nurse's uniform at The Uniform Shop, white pantyhose at Zellers and walking shoes at Sears. All cash purchases. Nothing to trace.

A cape would work better than a coat, for under it she could wear Mattie's old baby tote. Held snug against her chest, a newborn would be merely a bulge.

Lydia got her shoulder-length blond hair cut short and bought a pair of dark-rimmed dime-store glasses. With Lady Clairol's help, she could be brunette in half an hour.

Every couple of days Lydia walked past the Rendezvous Bar between eleven and one. Fiona was always there. She had acquired a baseball cap to hold the money people gave her. Lydia dropped in whatever she owed: forty dollars, sixty dollars, depending on how many days had gone by.

All was in readiness. By now the baby must be due. Each morning Lydia opened the newspaper to the Classified section. No birth announcement yet. Why didn't that damn baby get born? Or maybe it had been born, but Mrs. Shaw had not put in an announcement. That sure would wreck the best of plans. Lydia fretted, bit her nails, and got more nervous every day. And then, on December 5th, there it was:

Shaw. To Bill and Rita, a son, Daren Joseph, seven pounds, six ounces. Born December 4 at Grace Hospital. A brother for Emily and Sara.

Lydia's fingers jittered as she refolded the newspaper. At last the day of reckoning had come. The kitchen clock said 9:00. In two hours Fiona would be at her post, where she would remain until one o'clock. Lydia had plenty of time.

She phoned the hospital.

"Could you tell me Mrs. Rita Shaw's room number, please."

"Connell Wing, 16E."

After hanging up, Lydia repeated it to herself five times.

Then she went into the bathroom and got out the bottle of semi-permanent, dark brown dye. Comb in, leave on twenty minutes, wash off. Voilà! Instant brunette.

Ten minutes to dry and fluff her hair. No time to curl it. She got into her uniform and pinned on her badge. MARGARET McNEAL, R.N. Very professional. Then she did her makeup: foundation in a slightly darker shade, brown pencil to thicken her brows. The glasses gave a final touch.

Before leaving, she posed in front of her full-length mirror, looking at herself from the front, from over her left shoulder and then from over her right. Perfect. Lydia looked nothing like the sorrowing widow who had read her victim impact statement two months ago in Number One Courtroom.

Matthew and Mattie smiled. They were pleased too. She picked up their photograph and kissed it.

"Wish me luck."

She left her car in the parking lot across the street from the hospital. As she hurried along the sidewalk, her navy blue cape swirled about her ankles. Not so fast! She slowed her pace to a sedate walk. Look calm, she said to herself as she entered the lobby. Look calm yet worried. Pretend you're here to visit a sick friend.

She took the elevator to the basement. This was the tricky bit, leaving her cape and the baby tote in the washroom down the hall from the X-ray department. But this washroom got little use. She had checked that. People needing X-rays didn't make many bathroom stops. Maybe the nurses flushed them out before their journey to the bowels of the hospital.

Lydia hung up her cape and the tote on the hook on the back of the door, then stole a quick look at herself in the mirror over the wash basin. Uniform. Badge. Glasses. She looked like someone you'd trust with your life.

Then up the elevator to the fourth floor. Maternity was down the hall, turn right at the nursing station. The nurses had just carried the babies to their mothers. Perfect timing. Lydia walked purposefully along the corridor, past the premature nursery where, behind a glass wall, tiny wrinkled red creatures no bigger than puppies lay in their incubators, naked except for the tubes taped to their bodies. Lydia paused outside 16E, straightened her shoulders, took a deep breath and marched in.

The ward held four beds. As she entered the ward, four women looked up vaguely with bovine, luminous eyes. When Lydia approached Rita Shaw's bed, each of the others returned her attention to the blanketed bundle at her breast.

Lydia smiled. "Sorry, but I need to borrow your baby for half an hour. The doctor has ordered a few routine tests. Nothing to worry about."

"But my baby has been feeding for only five minutes!"

"He can finish when I bring him back. I'll make sure you get extra time with him."

With a soft pop, Mrs. Shaw detached the baby from her teat. The tiny lips continued to suck as Lydia took him into her arms. As she strode out of the ward, she felt Mrs. Shaw's eyes following her.

Left turn toward the elevators, past the nursing station. That was hurdle number one. But the two nurses who sat there continued to work on their charts as she went by. Next hurdle was the elevator, where two orderlies and a nurse waited with an unconscious patient on a stretcher. They all got onto the elevator ahead of Lydia, who squeezed in at one side. At the second floor the others got off. Lydia continued down to the basement.

Carrying the baby openly in her arms, she met no curious glances from the patients who sat waiting in the alcove outside the X-ray room. A white-coated technician who walked toward her, going the opposite direction, nodded curtly.

In the washroom, nothing had been disturbed. She put on the tote, then stuffed the baby into it, blanket and all. A small sigh. Probably he liked it there, dark and warm under the cape, close to her thudding heart.

The extra bulge on her chest was scarcely noticeable as long as she kept her shoulders hunched forward. Lydia took off her glasses, then used the stairs up to the lobby.

The lobby was crowded with people heading this way and that. Just inside the hospital entrance, two uniformed security guards chatted casually. Neither gave her a glance as the automatic door opened and she passed through.

Outside, a middle-aged woman stood beside a man in a wheelchair. A nurse, coatless despite the cold, was with them. A patient going home, Lydia guessed, waiting for his ride.

Twenty feet from the entrance, she passed a huddle of smokers, all leaning toward each other like members of a conspiracy. The two who wore stethoscopes had a particularly furtive air, as if they were even more anxious than Lydia to avoid observation.

She had left her car unlocked—one less thing to fiddle with. And the parking lot had no attendant. Lydia waited while a man got into a Volvo and drove away. Quickly, before anyone else came along, she undid her cape, pulled the baby out of the tote, and laid him on the car floor behind the driver's seat.

The baby whimpered. Probably he was cold, wrapped in one thin hospital blanket. She turned on the car heater full blast. Soothed by the motion of the car, he was asleep in less than the ten minutes it took her to drive home.

She put her car into the garage. With the car door and the garage door closed, no one would hear the baby if he started to cry. It wouldn't be for long—just long enough to shampoo most of the colour from her hair, rinse the shower stall, and shove the nurse's uniform, white shoes, badge, Clairol bottle and all the rest of that stuff into a pillow slip with a brick to weigh it down.

Hurry! Hurry! It was past ten thirty. By now someone must have noticed that Baby Boy Shaw was not with his mother, not having tests, and not in the newborn nursery. The search would be on. The police might already know.

She drove right out of town, heading north through Claxtons Corners and Newburgh until she came to the old bridge where County Road Six crossed the Onondaga River. She stopped on the bridge. There was no other car in sight when she heaved the pillow case over the railing. The river was deep here, and she was twenty miles from town.

On her way back to the city, Lydia turned on the car radio to drown out the baby's wails. Twelve noon. She switched to the local station for the news. Wars, bombings, robberies. No abductions so far.

Fiona, wrapped in a black leather jacket five sizes too large, sat in her usual place on the sidewalk outside the Rendezvous Bar. When Lydia beckoned from the car, she stuffed her baseball cap into her gym bag and got to her feet. Lydia reached across to open the passenger door.

"Get in."

Fiona heard the wails. "So you got the baby?"

"Yes. He's on the floor in the back."

"That's a funny place to put a baby." Half rising, Fiona twisted in her seat to get a look.

"Sit down, for Pete's sake, and get your seatbelt on."

"Afraid the cops will stop us?"

Lydia snapped, "I've better things to spend my money on than traffic fines."

"Then you better slow down. This is a sixty kilometre zone."

She touched her foot to the brake. This was no time to get nervous.

Mrs. Nagbor's basement apartment had its entrance through the side door and down a flight of steps from the landing. The main room, which held a sofa, a coffee table and a television, had a small L-shaped kitchen off the far end. From it one door led to the bathroom and another to the bedroom, where Mrs. Nagbor had set up a wooden crib against the wall opposite the bed.

"Where's the phone?" Fiona asked after her inspection was complete.

"No phone."

"What if you want to call me?"

"I won't."

Lydia ignored the smile that twitched at the corner of Fiona's mouth. "Everything you need is here," she said brusquely. Food. Formula. Baby supplies. As soon as I leave, you'd better feed him. The instructions are right on the formula package." She set the baby on the sofa and opened her purse. "Here's your key to the apartment."

"Okay."

Lydia pulled a fat envelope from her purse. "Here's $1,500 in twenty dollar bills. That's one month's pay in advance. If you need to buy anything, use this money and keep receipts so I can reimburse you."

"When will you be back?"

"In about a month."

"That's a long time."

"I'm going to visit relatives in England over Christmas. You're on your own."

Fiona was counting the money as Lydia left.

On her way home, Lydia stopped at The Bay to do some Christmas shopping. Cardigan for Dad, bath-and-beauty gift basket for Mom, scarf and gloves for Diane. That took an hour.

She was groping for her house key when the unmarked police car pulled into the driveway. Constable Burns and Staff Sergeant Wallace got out.

"What is it?" asked Lydia, careful to express surprise and concern. "Would you like to come in?"

Wallace was gravely polite, bending over backward not to sound suspicious as she described the abduction of Bill Shaw's baby.

"That's horrible," said Lydia. "One day old! Who could do such a thing?"

The officers wanted to know where Lydia had been all morning.

"I went shopping at The Bay."

"The Bay doesn't open until ten. What were you doing earlier? I'm sorry, but I must ask."

Wallace's soft West Indian voice invited confidence. Lydia saw no threat in the warm brown eyes, yet all at once she felt her breath stick in her throat like an egg she'd swallowed whole.

"I was home, washing my hair."

They said nothing about searching the house, but Lydia knew that would happen sooner or later. She wasn't afraid. The baby had not been here. They would find no evidence of Lydia's purchases or preparation, nothing that could to lead them to Fiona or to Mrs. Nagbor's basement apartment.

Lydia spent the next few days addressing Christmas cards and watching the TV news. She surfed the channels to catch Rita Shaw's tearful entreaty over and over again. "Please, please, bring my baby back!" It was on the local news and on the CBC. Even some U.S. newscasts picked it up.

Diane phoned, offered to visit. Lydia turned her down. The company of Matthew and Mattie was all she needed. Once again she felt included in their smiles.

She took the photograph with her when she went to Mom and Dad's place for Christmas. Diane, Joe and the boys were there too, all crowded into the big stone house at Lovatts Corners where Lydia and Diane had grown up.

Everyone pussyfooted around, unsure whether to mention Matthew and Mattie. Lydia overheard their whispered talk. Poor Lydia. The first Christmas after her great loss. How could she bear to sing carols, decorate the tree, smell the savory odour of roasting turkey?

Diane was the only one to see that, inexplicably, Lydia was coping well.

"You've changed," she said, "since October."

"I guess I was bound to. Like you said, I had to go through all those stages."

Diane looked perplexed. "You don't fit the pattern. Acceptance is a quiet, peaceful state. But you're as tight as a fiddle string." She looked at Lydia reflectively. "May I ask you a personal question?"

"Yes, but I may not answer it."

"Have you ... met someone?"

"Why would you think that?"

"You're so edgy and distracted. Half the time you don't hear when people talk to you."

"So you think I've fallen in love?"

"Well, it does happen. You're young."

Lydia shook her head. Even if she wanted to, she could not have described this new emotion. Excitement, rapture, a touch of fear. Falling in love had felt a bit like that. Or sex for the first time. But she'd never longed for love or sex the way she had longed for revenge.

Lydia didn't think that she was being followed. Yet how could she be sure? The middle of a police investigation was not a safe time to visit Mrs. Nagbor's apartment. But as the weeks went by, and the rent came due, and the advance on Fiona's wages ran out, Lydia had no choice.

The route she took was complex and circuitous. If another car had been trailing hers, she would have seen it long before she drew up in front of Mrs. Nagbor's house. She had the money with her. Her excuse for being late was all prepared.

But Fiona had gone.

"She live here one week," Mrs. Nagbor said, staring forlornly at her threadbare carpet. "Then she disappear. The baby too. I thought she go home to Momma and never come back. So I got new tenant." Mrs.

Nagbor's hands shook; she was trembling throughout her body.

Why, she's afraid, Lydia thought. She thinks she's in trouble because she rented the apartment to someone else after I'd paid two months' rent.

"I give you back the money," Mrs. Nagbor mumbled.

"This is very serious." With an effort, Lydia kept her voice stern and righteous. "You broke the law by taking a new tenant. What's even worse ..." She leaned forward menacingly. "I suspect that your apartment is illegal."

A moan came from Mrs. Nagbor's throat. She pressed her palms together and moved her lips in prayer, or so it appeared, for the words were not English.

"I'll tell you what," said Lydia, "I won't report you. But if the police come, tell them that the girl and the baby were never here. You never saw ..."

Mrs. Nagbor looked up, her pale eyes terrified. "The police!" she cried as she crossed herself. "I never have trouble before."

Lydia got to her feet. When she reached the doorway, she halted and turned to Mrs. Nagbor.

"Remember. The girl with the baby was never here. Do not say a word."

Lydia did not expect to find Fiona at Wellington Square. Nor had she any idea what she might learn from the youth who huddled on the sidewalk outside the Rendezvous Bar. She didn't recall having seen him before, although she did recognize the black leather jacket, which was as small on him as it had been large on Fiona. Three inches of bare arm showed above his wrists.

"I'm looking for information." When Lydia pulled out a ten dollar bill, the boy's eyes brightened. "There's a girl I want to find. She used to hang out here. Short, very thin. Black lipstick. Black eyeliner. Whole bunch of hoops piercing her right ear. Her name's Fiona."

"Fiona!" The boy laughed.

"That may not be her real name."

"None of us use real names."

"But you do know her? Can you tell me where she is?"

Lydia put the bill into his hand.

"Got another of those?"

"If you tell me."

He looked at her coolly. "The money first." Lydia handed it over.

"She came by here a couple weeks before Christmas. Said she was going to Vancouver, or maybe San Francisco."

"Alone?"

"Yeah."

"She didn't have a baby with her?"

The youth squinted. "I don't remember."

Lydia pulled out another ten. "Will this help your memory?"

"A couple more will help."

She gave him a twenty. "Okay. Was there a baby?"

"No."

This was like stuffing money into a parking metre. He got fifty bucks from her before she drew the line.

"You get the rest when you've told the whole story. It's worth another fifty bucks to me."

"Not much to tell. She said she'd had a baby, but she'd sold it. A friend of hers looked up private adoptions on the Internet. He posted this baby on the Web site. In a couple of weeks this foreign guy showed up and paid her twenty thou for the kid. That's why she had to leave town. There's a law against selling babies, you know."

Lydia gave him the fifty. "What name did she use around here?"

"That's worth another fifty."

"Not to me it isn't." She shut her purse. "Have a good day."

The sun was shining as she drove out of the parking lot under Wellington Square. It was one of those late January thaws, with their false promise of spring in the air.

Time to get on with her life. The price of Matthew's and Mattie's deaths had been paid. Not the full price, but more than she had bargained for. Bill Shaw would never see his child.

The heavy weight of grief had been lifted from her shoulders. What she felt was not quite happiness, but a promise of its possibility. When she got home, she'd phone Diane. If Joe could look after the boys for a week, she'd treat her sister to a holiday in Bermuda. Images of tennis courts and beaches rose in her mind as she drove up Wyandotte Avenue.

A Murder Coming
by James Powell

Since 1968, James Powell has published more than one hundred finely crafted short stories. Each tale takes months of work and is meticulously polished. Jim's stories are frequently comic, but just as often are wound around a particularly dark core. In 1990, fourteen of his best works were collected in a book with the same title as this story. A new collection is forthcoming in 2005. A twelve-time finalist for the Crime Writers of Canada's Arthur Ellis Award for Best Short Story, Jim won the award in 2003. His winning story, "Bottom Walker," was originally published in *Ellery Queen Mystery Magazine* and was reprinted in the Insomniac Press anthology *Hard Boiled Love*.

Fog is always over there and never here. When the man in the fur-collared overcoat and homburg reached the CNR tracks, the fog had moved to the edge of the lake. When he reached the lake and the sagging wharf, the fog stood a bit off from shore.

For a moment the man stared fretfully out across the water. Then he noticed someone on the edge of the fog at the end of the wharf and quickly picked his way out to him. "Did Alcott send you for me?" he asked. "My name is Watford."

The other man was staring down into a rowboat. He looked up slowly. His face was broad and stubbled with white. "No," he said. His breath smelled of alcohol.

"Damn!" muttered Watford and hurled a ball of paper off into the fog. ("Would you mind delivering this, Judge?" the station-master had asked, handing Watford his own telegram in which he had answered Alcott's curious wire and announced his arrival time.) The fine, drifting rain had started up again. "Five dollars to row me out there," said Watford. The man looked at him with soft unblinking eyes. Watford drew a banknote from his wallet and held it under the man's nose. "If you don't know where Alcott's place is, I can show you," he said.

"Not many people on the islands this time of year," said the man.

"Five dollars," said Watford, who didn't care to discuss the comings and goings of a future provincial Minister of Justice with a local inhabitant.

The man shrugged and tucked the money in a pocket of his mackinaw. He stepped down into the boat and drew it up tight against the pilings.

With a strong hand under Watford's elbow he helped—almost lifted—him down. Then, as his passenger arranged himself in the stern, the man untied the boat and pushed off. Before the oars were in their locks the fog had closed in and the wharf had disappeared.

Now nothing was visible beyond the boat except a dark rim of water tufted with mist. At intervals shapes emerged from the fog and then slipped back into it. Watford, who felt the cold off the water almost at once, hunched inside his coat and thought of crocodiles and Loch Ness. "Your boat's taking water," he said suddenly, noticing the water lapping around his dapper little feet.

The man at the oars had been watching him with an expression as placid as a cow's. Now he shook his head.

"Don't tell me all this is from the rain," insisted Watford.

The man shook his head. "The boat's taking water."

"That's what I said," snapped Watford.

The man shook his head again. "It's not my boat."

Watford frowned. "Well, we could still use a can or something to bail with," he said uneasily.

"Try your hat," the man suggested.

As he groped for a cutting reply, it occurred to Watford that the man wasn't staring so much as offering his face to be recognized. "Have you and I met before?" he asked.

"You once sentenced me to be hanged, Judge," said the man. "If you call that a meeting."

Watford leaned forward curiously, searching the slack cheeks, the pitted skin, the water-blue eyes. The man grinned shyly. Then, holding the oars in his armpits, he took a drink from a bottle in a brown paper bag. Watford refused the offered bottle with a disdainful shake of the head. Then he shook his head again, perplexed.

The man started to row again. "Edward McSorley," he said.

"Ah, yes," said Watford. In the late forties McSorley, a small-town hardware-store owner, had been convicted of the murder of his wife. In the course of the trial it was also revealed that the McSorleys were The Shouting Bandits, bank robbers whose brief career had made them the darlings of the southern Ontario press. In fact, McSorley claimed that his wife wasn't dead but had run off with their accumulated loot.

Abruptly, Watford gave a dry laugh. "McSorley, do you remember the witness, the neighbour who saw you through the window come up behind your wife that night and choke her with your arm? Do you remember how you answered him when you took the stand? You said—"

"My wife is a judo expert," repeated McSorley gravely. "I often let her practise on me after dinner."

Watford forced a frown. "Not that I approved the commuting of your sentence, McSorley," he said. "The death penalty is a last bastion of the grand style in this all-too-colourless world. In his heart even the simplest of murderers sees the justice of an eye for an eye. Isn't that so?"

"Don't look at me. I didn't kill my wife," said McSorley.

"I had hoped we could speak frankly," said Watford. "After all, you've served your time." He paused. "You have, haven't you?"

"Twenty-five years," said McSorley, peering over his shoulder into the fog.

"Good for you," said Watford. "But now that the time has come to rehabilitate yourself, here's a tip: talk about the bloody deed at the drop of a hat. I mean it. If you ask me, our prisons should emphasize the teaching of communications skills—public speaking, first-person narrative, dramatic reading with gestures and all. You see, so few of us actually get to kill in white heat. The man on the street thirsts to know what it's like. I confess to a certain curiosity myself."

McSorley rested on his oars. "Maudie's still alive," he said. "And the only thing I learned in prison was this." He lunged forward, a hunting knife in his upraised hand. Wide-eyed with fear, Watford fell backward across the stern. The knife arced down and stopped just short of his throat. "I learned you don't do it like that," said McSorley. With one hand he pulled Watford back into his seat. "You come up like this." He arced the knife up from the bottom of the boat and pressed it against Watford's stomach. "Want me to go through that one more time?" he asked earnestly. "Are you sure you got it?"

"I got it," said Watford.

McSorley looked at him doubtfully. After a moment he said, "I guess you'd better do some bailing." Watford crushed his homburg into a scoop and started throwing water over the side. McSorley watched, mildly interested, lounging back on his seat, legs crossed and an elbow on the gunwale. He took a drink, then another,

Watford bailed. "You have to admit you had a fair trial," he said hurriedly, regretting the squeak in his voice. "Eminently fair as I recall. The evidence was all there. Oh, perhaps Brownish could have made more of prosecution's failure to positively identify those bone fragments in the incinerator as your wife's."

"He giggled a lot," McSorley said.

"Yes," panted Watford as he bailed, "Brownish was famous for his little giggling fits in the courtroom. But he came from a fine family. We all forgave him a lot for that. Poor Brownish. He died several years ago, or perhaps you hadn't heard. Walked into an open manhole in broad daylight."

The boat was now bailed out. Watford's fingers were like sticks from the cold. The icy water had set his wrists aching. He started to throw the sodden wreckage of his hat over the side.

But McSorley wagged the knife. "Why don't you put it on?" he said.

Watford did. The leather sweatband made him shiver. Water trickled down his face and the back of his neck. He had the sudden urge to cry.

"Here's to Brownish," said McSorley, raising the bottle to his lips. "We're having a wonderful time and wish he was here." The he handed the bottle to the unhappy Watford.

Watford braced himself, tilted the bottle, and choked in surprise. "Cognac?" he asked hoarsely, pulling down the bag to read the label.

"Special occasion," said McSorley.

As he handed the bottle back, Watford remembered with a start that it was Alcott who had prosecuted McSorley's case. He cleared his throat nervously and said, "Say, is this what you read about in books where the released murderer hunts down the person he's supposed to have killed and then murders him before the very eyes of the judge and prosecutor who convicted him? The ironic part, you see, is that he can't be tried twice for the same crime." He added almost hopefully, "Is that what all this is about?"

"I couldn't kill anybody," said McSorley. "I'm just not a violent person. Now, Maudie is a violent person. Once I saw her break a man's nose with her forearm." McSorley looked at the knife as though seeing it for the first time. He offered it to Watford. "Here," he said sheepishly, handing the judge the knife.

Watford's heart pounded. Was it a trick? He had to force himself to take the knife. Had McSorley just wanted to humiliate him? Clenching the knife, Watford looked the man in the eye defiantly and swept the wet Homburg off his head and over the side. McSorley grinned meekly.

Breathing easier now, Watford said, "All right, let's get going. We can't sit here all afternoon." Watford had never ordered anyone to do something at knifepoint before. He found it strangely exhilarating. Frightened, he pushed the knife deep in his pocket and folded his arms. "What is it you want, McSorley?" he demanded.

McSorley rowed in silence. Finally he said, "At the trial nobody asked why we were called The Shouting Bandits."

"It was hardly relevant," said Watford. A small island with a single pine tree slid by in the fog. Alcott's island wasn't far now. "Proceed," said Watford. "Consider yourself asked."

"I guess the first time I met my wife is the best place to begin," said

McSorley. "She was the new bank teller just arrived in town that day, a big-boned, broad-shouldered woman with this hard-of-hearing problem and a voice like a bugle. But too vain to wear a hearing aid. Funny, because she was plain as a post. Kicked out of the School of Library Science at the University of Western Ontario because of it—her hearing, not her looks." He faltered. "I'm not telling it right," he said helplessly. "I guess prisons should teach those communications skills you talked about."

McSorley pulled on the oars thoughtfully, as though ordering things in his mind. "Hardware stores smell like courtrooms, all paper and dried-up ink."

"More matter and less art, McSorley," said Watford.

"When my turn came at the teller's window that first day, Maudie blared right out, 'Speak up there, Mr. Man. You're not in church,'" said McSorley in a rush. "Everybody turned. The bank manager stuck his head out of his cubbyhole. But what really hit me like a load of bricks was that she was right. I mean I had been whispering in the bank all my life and so had my father before me.

"The next day, Sunday, I spent walking the few streets of the town trying to figure out what to do. After two generations of whispering how could I put things right and become my own man again? All of a sudden there was Maudie coming out of the Fallows Tourist Rooms carrying a fibre suitcase. The bank had fired her and she was going home to Sarnia.

"Well, there weren't any busses on Sundays, so I offered to drive her. It was in the car that I laughed and shouted and guessed the only way for me to get my own back was to rob the bank. Maudie punched my arm and shouted that was the best damn idea she'd ever heard and to count her in. She felt banks had given her a raw deal. And libraries, too. But we both agreed there was more money in robbing banks.

"The next thing I knew I was visiting Maudie regularly in Sarnia where we'd sit around and shout about robbing banks. You wouldn't really think that could lead to wedding bells, but it did. On our honeymoon we sneaked back to town in masks and robbed the bank. That's when she broke the bank manager's nose. He didn't jump when she shouted, 'Jump!' A violent person, Maudie.

"For the next few months, Mondays meant close up the hardware store and rob a bank. But I'd had my fill. Nothing makes you speak right up in a bank like knowing you've robbed it. Besides, I was elected captain of the Northside River Street Merchants hockey team with Monday practices and a good chance that year of beating our Southside rivals. So I said, 'Hold the phone, Maudie.'

"She didn't like that a bit. I could hear it in her voice after dinner when she'd get me in a full nelson, snap my neck, and say, 'Tomorrow we're going to rob a bank. One and done.' 'No, now Maudie,' I'd say, 'enough's enough.' But love curdles fast when you've built a marriage on robbing banks."

"So you say she took all the money and ran," said Watford. "But why make it look as if you'd killed her?"

"Because I'm somebody to be reckoned with," insisted McSorley. "I robbed banks just because I whispered in them. She had to be afraid of what a guy like that would do if she stole his share. So you were supposed to kill me. But you didn't."

"God knows I tried," said Watford. "I wasn't the one who commuted your sentence."

"Anyway, the big question now in her mind is what a guy like me is going to do to make up for those twenty-five long years I spent in jail," said McSorley.

"So you've really found her then," said Watford.

"I put a private detective on that," said McSorley. "She owns a place called Echo Lake Lodge about forty miles from here—just a couple of ratty cabins for fishermen and a three-stool lunch counter." He smiled. "Tell you what I did. When I got out I bought an old car and paid her a visit, just a wave and a smile and hanging around outside. Just giving her the jumps."

A dark shelf loomed ahead of them in the fog. Alcott's landing. "If that's what this is all about, I wouldn't advise you trying to harass Mr. Alcott and myself," warned Watford. "We have friends with the police who'd be happy to extend themselves on our behalf."

"I'm not going to bother you anymore, Judge. Honest," promised McSorley. "Just let me finish what I was telling you. You see, I knew she couldn't take much of the waiting and wondering what I was going to do. She'd have to come after me. And so there she was, padlocking the lunch-counter door behind her and there I was driving off in a cloud of dust. I let her chase me until I caught her, Judge. Now I've got her where she can't get away."

"Why tell me all this?" demanded Watford.

McSorley edged the boat up against the landing. "Because you're a judge," he said. "Because you say when people have the right to kill and when they don't."

"I've already told you you've got a murder coming, so to speak," said Watford, standing up.

McSorley helped him out of the boast and onto the landing. "The trouble is I'm just not a violent person," he said. "But I let her chase me until she could taste my blood and then I put her where she couldn't get away. When the police come looking, they'll find her. Or her body."

Watford looked down at him. "Her body?" he asked.

McSorley grinned. "Well, you see, Judge, I told her a lie. I told her I'd hired a couple of guys to kill her."

"Figuring on scaring her to death?" asked Watford contemptuously. He stuffed his hands in his pockets and started to walk away. Then he stopped and pulled out the knife. "Here. This is yours," he said.

But McSorley had already pushed off. "That's all right," McSorley said gravely. "You just remember what I told you." He arced his fist down. "Not like that. Like this." He arced his fist up. "Mr. Alcott never did get that straight."

Watford gave a puzzled frown. Then something moved in the fog. Someone was coming down the landing toward him. "Alcott?" he called doubtfully, for Alcott was a small man with a quick step.

"Alcott?" he called again.

McSorley rested his oars and sat there on the edge of the fog. He held up the bottle in a little salute and before putting it to his lips said, "You'll have to shout louder than that, Judge. A lot louder than that."

Bush Fever

by Peter Sellers

Since 1987, Peter Sellers has edited more than a dozen anthologies of Canadian crime fiction, including *Iced* and *Hard Boiled Love* with Kerry J. Schooley for Insomniac Press. A regular contributor to *Ellery Queen Mystery Magazine*, his story "Avenging Miriam" won the 2001 EQMM Readers Award. Since publishing his first stories in *Mike Shayne Mystery Magazine*, Peter's work has appeared in *Alfred Hitchcock Mystery Magazine*, *Hardboiled* and in numerous anthologies.

They said the hammer went into his head like a howitzer shell, smashing the face and crushing the skull.

His death had been quick, they said, but it had also been painful. Lying gasping in the mud with the hammer sticking out from under him like a withered limb. The nearest doctor an hour away. The nearest hospital three.

He and Marco worked noon till midnight, and Blake and I came on for the graveyard shift. It was Marco who was swinging the hammer, slamming it on the end of a length of pipe that Tom held pressed against the jammed piston. When Marco's foot slipped in the slick mud that spilled from the drill, his massive arms and shoulders drove the hammer into Tom instead.

The truck pitched and shuddered along the rutted road, headlights darting wildly into the darkness as if desperately seeking shelter. Blake always took the road too fast and it slammed me against the door so the handle dug into my side and then tossed me back against Blake so his elbow made it equal. In the distance, the drilling rig stood bathed in light and reminded me, as it had the first time, of something dropped down from outer space into Alberta's vast and empty north.

As soon as we climbed out of the truck we knew something was wrong. There wasn't the usual activity. We found them behind the rig. Tom was already dead, covered up by the geologist's coat. Marco sat on the ground a few feet away, hands on his knees, empty-eyed.

"Is he dead?" Blake asked, although it seemed pretty obvious to me. Brady, the geologist, nodded and Blake took off his hard hat. "Jesus," he said.

I went over to Marco whose eyes bored sightlessly into the night. "Christ, Marco. Can I get you something?"

"I slipped," he said, not looking at me. He was covered in mud. "He's dead." I wasn't clear whether he was asking or telling me. But I told him yes and left him in his shock.

The ambulance came soon after. The driver saying it was just as well Tom was dead because, if he hadn't been, the ride to the hospital would have finished him off with a lot more suffering than he'd probably felt.

Tom's body, the ambulance and the local Mounties were gone by four in the morning. The cops took Marco for questioning, but Blake said it was just a formality. Blake watched as their tail lights disappeared over the first rise of land, then Brady came up to us. "Let's go," he said.

"Whatcha mean?" I asked.

Blake just shrugged and put his hard hat back on.

The geologist looked at me like I was an idiot. "Let's get this drill operational."

"We had a man get stove in here, Brady," I said. "You expect us to work on like he got a hangnail or something?"

"We're close," Brady said. "And the sooner we get there the sooner we can shut this rig down, move on and start somewhere else." He pointed at Blake. "He's been around long enough to understand that. So get 'er pumping, boys. Now." He turned and walked away.

"Well," I said, "you wanna hold or you wanna swing?"

Blake gave me a grin that took all the cold out of the night and put it in my chest as he reached for the hammer.

We fixed the pump and brought the well in and capped it without us seeing Drop One of oil. Each time that happened, even after three months on the rigs, it still flooded me with disappointment. I'd been raised on old movie scenes of men rushing around in a shower of crude as the black gold rained down from gushers spouting a hundred feet in the air. That image had been stuck in my mind when I signed on as a roughneck.

Blake bounced us back to town. Apache Drilling put us up at the local hotel near wherever the mobile rig was located at the time and paid for our room, breakfast and dinner. That was about all we had time for, working twelve-hour shifts twenty-one days straight and then getting four days off.

The hotel room had a bed, chair, rickety table and wallpaper with historic oil wells on it. The bathroom was shared by the hall and, since most of us were roughnecks, the ring was permanent and black as crude. If they'd been smart, they'd've enamelled the fixtures black.

I scrubbed the grime off as best I could and met Blake in the saloon for a beer. It was the first time he wanted to talk about what happened.

"Bush fever," he said as he sucked the foam off his fourth draft. "It gets to you sometime when you're out there too long. You can see it in the eyes."

"See what?"

"Being alone in the middle of nowhere with that drill working and you a slave to it. It reaches inside you after a while. And your mind just goes away every now and then."

I tried to remember what I'd seen in Marco's eyes at the rig, but I wasn't sure it looked like what Blake was describing or not. "Is that what happened to Marco?"

Blake swished a mouthful of beer around and thought about this for a moment, then swallowed. "Naw. He just slipped." He laughed. "Hell, couple times up there I nearly slipped and took your head with me."

It somehow didn't strike me funny.

Next morning, the desk clerk at the hotel called me as I went down to breakfast. "You know that guy got killed yesterday? What should I do with his stuff?"

"What stuff?"

"We hadda clean out his room. Got a bag full of personal stuff here, and I wanna know what I should do with it."

"How the hell should I know? Didn't somebody from the company call you?"

"Nope." He held the brown grocery bag toward me with both hands. "You worked with him, and I got no address to send it, so if you don't take it I'll toss it."

I took it. Tom wasn't leaving much of a legacy. There was a wind-up watch that didn't wind, a ring of unidentified keys, some socks and underwear and a flannel shirt he'd loved so much it was worn thin enough to see through. There was no cash, of course, and I wondered who I'd see wearing the rest of his clothes and a pair of western boots I recalled him wearing in the saloon a night or two. At the bottom of the bag, there were photographs of two women. One of them I recognized. On the back it said simply, "Sarah" and "15".

That could have been her age, but I doubted it. There was only one hotel in town so I climbed the stairs to the next floor. The door to Room 15 was ajar. Through the crack I could se her packing clothes in a well-travelled trunk. She turned toward me when I pushed the half-open door wide.

"Sarah?" I said.

She gave me a long steady look, frozen in the act of folding a nightgown that would have been totally useless in the face of a northern Alberta winter. "I've seen you around," she said.

"My name's Cole. I worked the rig with Tom. Well, we worked different shifts, but the same rig."

She went back to folding. "Funny choice of name for a guy working an oil rig."

It wasn't the first time that had been pointed out. She placed a dull patterned dress on top of the negligee. "Were you there when Tom was killed?"

"You know about it, then?"

"Place like this, you know how word gets around, Cole." She put a pair of patched jeans on top of everything else and closed the lid. It was too full and the latches stayed about two inches apart.

"Is there anything I can do?" I asked.

"Help me get this closed."

I walked around the trunk and sat on it next to her. Our combined weight forced the lid down and I reached first between my legs and then between hers to snap the latches shut. She touched my knee

"Are you okay?" I asked her.

She looked puzzled for a moment and then she laughed. "You think Tom and I were lovers."

It was my turn to be puzzled. "Weren't you?"

He shook her head. "No. Marco and I had been, but never Tom."

"Marco?"

"Don't look so surprised. Marco is an attractive man in his own way. He's a few years older than me, but so what? After I broke it off, Tom was ready to step in, if I'd let him. He was a few years younger than me. What difference does it make?"

It didn't, and I said so. "Did Marco think you and Tom were lovers?"

She shrugged. "I know Blake joked about it a few times to Marco in the saloon, but I hardly knew what Marco was thinking even when we were together. Your guess is as good as mine. What difference does it make?" she asked again. "Anyway," she continued, "Tom had nothing to do with me leaving Marco."

"Did Marco know that?"

"I don't think he killed Tom on purpose, if that's what you mean." She stood. "Anyway, I've got a bus. Help me down with this."

The bus stop was outside a five-and-dime that had a lunch counter running the length of it. Sarah perched on a stool at the end near the window so she could see the bus before it pulled up. I set the trunk on its end next to her. "Can I buy you a coffee?" I asked.

She shrugged. The coffee was not worth drinking, so the mugs stood barely touched in front of us until they went cold. We didn't say anything until the bus arrived ten minutes later. I picked up the trunk again and half dragged it outside.

She bought a ticket from the driver, and he ticked the trunk in the luggage compartment.

"I'm sorry about Tom," I said as she prepared to board.

She shook her head. "Don't tell that to me. It doesn't matter. His mother is the one you should tell."

I got the name and address of Tom's mother from the head office of Apache Drilling. In case of accidents, such as Tom's, they always made you put next-of-kin down on the hiring documents. When I asked the girl on the other end of the line for information she didn't even ask why I wanted to know. That made me feel a little uneasy, as if things like this happened all too often.

Tom's mother lived in a small apartment above a convenience store in Edmonton. I rode the bus down three hours with Tom's few possessions in a mended duffel bag on the rack above my head. It slid back and forth as the bus climbed up and down through the foothills.

For some reason, I figured Tom's mother would know about his death. In retrospect, given the way Apache operated, there was no reason why I should have made that assumption. After all, no one else had come forward to claim his things.

As soon as I knocked on the door and she opened it and peered out above the chain I could tell she didn't know. "Yes?" she asked, brushing a wisp of hair back from her forehead.

"My name's Cole. I worked with Tom."

The door closed, the chain dropped, and the door opened again. "What happened?" She wore a snug pair of faded men's jeans and a plaid work shirt that fit her loosely. She must have been very young when Tom was born, for she looked not much older than Sarah.

"It was an accident. On the rig."

She nodded as if she had expected this and stood back to wave me into the apartment. "Please sit down."

Again, she brushed the hair back from her face. It was ginger and streaked lightly with grey, giving her the colouring of a tabby. She had freckles too, which formed a girlish cluster about her nose. "Coffee? Or a beer?"

Like Sarah, she was calm where I had expected hysterics. The death of a son always seemed to me something any parent would be distraught over. As if reading my thoughts, she handed me a beer and said, "I'll cry when you leave, but not until I know what happened."

I explained to her, as simply as possible, how the drill pipe fills with mud as it skewers deeper and deeper and how the pump clears that mud out as steadily as it comes in. If the pump's piston jams in the cylinder, drilling has to stop. And the fastest way to fix things is for one man to hold a length of steel pipe against the jammed piston head and another to hit the pipe as hard as he can with a sledge hammer. Jarring the piston loose again.

As I told her she watched my face intently as if she could see the words coming out and scrutinize them for signs that they lied. In the end, when she saw that they didn't, she slumped back in her chair. "Oh, Tommy," she whispered.

"I brought you his things."

"Thank you." She made no motion to take them from me so I set them gently on the coffee table.

"He was my only child," she said then. "He would have been about your age, and he always wanted to work on the oil rigs. I didn't want that, though. I wanted something better, but there comes a time when what your child wants matters more than what you want and I couldn't stop him. His father worked on the rigs, you see.

"I was fifteen when Tommy was born. His father was two years older. We ran away and lied about our ages and got married in Minneapolis. I never doubted that he loved me, but I wanted my son to have a better life, and when Tommy was born I had to choose, you see. I had to choose between my husband and my son. And I chose to take Tommy away from the oil fields. And away from his father.

"He was very angry. I suppose that's understandable. He blamed the boy for coming between us. I suppose that's understandable, too. I tried to stay in touch. I sent pictures and letters talking about Tommy, hoping his father would change. I never heard anything back but I never stopped writing until a couple of years ago when the letters and pictures started coming back Address Unknown. I don't even know if he ever got any of them at all.

"Tommy never knew his father, you see. That's why he wanted to work the oil fields. So he could find some sense of the man his father was." She gazed at me with such intensity that I had to look away.

"Would you like to see him?" she asked, and went to an old sideboard in the dining room and took out a photo album. It fell open, as if by an invisible hand, and she pointed to a picture of a darkly handsome young man who did not smile. It was faded and about twenty years old, but the face was unmistakable.

I must have stared at it for a long time because she said to me, "Is anything wrong?"

"Did Tom ever see that photo?"

She smiled a sweet, sad smile. "I never showed it to him," she said.

Blake was sitting in the same spot in the saloon when I got back. There was a half-empty draft glass in front of him and, for all I knew, he might never have moved.

"Where you been?" he asked.

"Went looking for Tom's mother." I sat down.

"Find her?"

"Yes." The waitress brought me two drafts as a reflex. "Sarah said you joked with Marco that she'd left him for Tom."

"A time or two, I guess." He signalled for more beer.

"How did Marco take it?"

Blake smiled. "He got real steamed. I've known him a long while, but I don't think I ever seen him so heated up."

"It must be tough," I said. "A lonely man thinking he'd lost his woman to a guy young enough to be his son. That'd work on your mind like bush fever, wouldn't you think?"

Blake just shrugged and I changed the subject. "By the way," I asked, "before he died, did you tell Tom that you were his father?"

Blake's glass stopped before it reached his lips. "I don't know what the hell you're talking about," he said quietly. "But one thing I do know, me and Marco worked these rigs years together. We fixed them pumps maybe thirty times. Maybe forty." He flicked the edge of his glass with a fingernail and it made a soft ping. "And Marco always put that sledge right where he wanted."

An Eye for an Eye
by Nancy Kilpatrick

As one of Canada's leading authors of dark fantasy fiction, Nancy creates noir with a distinctive bite. Her works includes the contemporary vampire classics *Near Dark* and the *Power of the Blood* series, currently republished by Mosaic Press. Although best known for her horror writing, as well as her *Darker Passions* novels under the name Amarantha Knight, Nancy is no stranger to crime fiction. She won the Arthur Ellis Award for Best Short Story in 1993 for her work "Mantrap." Nancy's latest book is another exercise in exploring the dark side. *The Goth Bible* was published this fall by St. Martin's Press.

Alexander Mifflin was stabbing my mother as my brother Bill and I walked in the back door. I dropped the Eatons shopping bags I carried and screamed. Last-minute gifts tumbled into the pools of bloody mincemeat. Mifflin turned. He and Bill fought. Bill outweighed him; he had wrestled at college. I rushed to my mother's blood-soaked body. The knife was lodged in her eye and, desperate, I yanked it out. Mother died in my arms seconds before Bill brought her killer to the ground. Before I could dial 911. Before she could say goodbye.

I know what you're thinking, the same thing the media is saying—I'm a psychopath. What makes me believe I have the right to be judge, jury and executioner? Your silly questions have nothing to do with me. I have that right by virtue of the fact that I have fought to stay alive in the face of shattering despair. You know yourself, it's survival of the fittest. You've thought that, even if you can't bring yourself to admit such a politically incorrect idea. I was a woman with a mission. Mission accomplished. If you'll hear me out, I know you'll understand.

Four years after my mother's death I came to the conclusion that murder is not so terrible. We all die anyway so what's it matter when or how? That might seem a jaded statement, but you know in your heart you've thought the same thing. We all have. It follows then that if one murderer can get off virtually scot-free, why not another? Why not me?

I used to believe in divine justice. Then I grew up. For a while I had faith in our man-made justice system. When that failed, when jurisprudence let a guilty man walk away with his freedom and my mother's blood on his hands, I grew up some more.

Who would avenge my mother? Who would stop that madman from repeating his crime against humanity? No one. No one but me.

Let me start closer to the beginning, the easiest place to try to make sense of me and my "crime," although there's no sense to *his* senseless crime.

The evidence was tangible, not circumstantial: Alexander Mifflin, a thirty-five-year-old Caucasian male broke into our North Vancouver home on Christmas Eve, ostensibly to steal anything of value. My mother was preparing mincemeat pies for the holiday dinner the next day. The lights were out in the rest of the house. Apparently she had been working in the kitchen and, when the sun set, turned on only one light. He surprised her there. She fought him—she was a large, strongly built woman of Scandinavian ancestry who did not give herself over easily to being intimidated. No one would have ever called her a coward. Neither is her daughter.

It was obvious they struggled. Chairs were overturned; the floor was a sea of mincemeat. A paring knife lay on the table to trim crusts, but he reached to the white-ash knife rack and pulled out a Henckel with a six-inch blade. Mother always loved good knives and had the blades honed by the man with the knife-sharpening cart who came by weekly. The coroner commented on the sharpness of the blade, because the twenty-eight stab wounds were, for the most part, clean. There were seven in her chest, two in her stomach, one in her left leg. The knife penetrated her diaphragm. She was left-handed and that side received the worst treatment. But the majority of the stab wounds were to her back, puncturing both lungs, one kidney, and, because the blade was so long, her heart. The most gruesome sight was to her left eye, where I found the knife lodged. The blade had pierced her brain. As I withdrew it, pale matter seeped from the wound. I can still see the tissue, like wood pulp.

I lived in a state of numbed grief. At the funeral I couldn't cry. Later, when we sold the house, before I left for college, as Bill and I sorted through my mother's belongings and I asked for her knives, he stopped and advised me, "Connie, try to forget what happened and get on with your life." But how could I forget?

No fourteen-year-old should have to experience what I did. Unless you've seen death close up, you cannot know how shocking it is. When the body seems to sigh. When the light fades blue-lace crystal eyes to flat dull agates. When a kind of gas—maybe the spirit—wafts from an open mouth and ascends, rippling the air. My mother was gone. Her murderer would pay.

But he did not pay. Four years passed before Mifflin came to trial. I waited patiently through the delays, the motions and counter motions. He opted for judge only, no jury, knowing that ordinary people would find his acts against my mother incomprehensible. Still, through my frozen grief, I had faith.

But he'd had a bad childhood, a therapist testified, and had paid in advance. A minister assured the court that Mifflin attended church, helped out in the community, would be missed. He was a father, out of work, with a lovely wife and children to support. Not a crazed dope fiend, but a decent man, just desperate, said his brother. A police officer reported he'd been a suspect in several crimes and charged with burglary once before, but those charges had been dropped for lack of evidence. The court ruled that information inadmissible. Mifflin testified he did not recall reaching for the knife. He did not realize he stabbed my mother. Twenty-eight times. When I pulled the knife from my mother's brain, effectively I destroyed his fingerprints.

All throughout the trial I felt nothing, just stared at Mifflin, memorizing how he looked, his mannerisms, and finally his cursory testimony. The entire process had been like mining a vein that turned out to be corrupted. And the further along we travelled, the worse it got. The delays only helped his case. And the deals. Not murder one for Mr. Mifflin, who pleaded guilty, but manslaughter. Twenty years. He had already served four, he would be eligible for parole after another six.

The system failed me. But I vowed not to fail my mother.

How do you kill a murderer? It's not as easy as one might think. It takes a lot of planning. Alexander Mifflin was paranoid—he assumed everyone had an intent as evil as his own. I understand paranoia. I've lived with it since that Christmas Eve. I have not felt safe since because there are other Alexander Mifflins in the world and you never know when they will invade the privacy of your home and take control of your life and stab you or a loved one to death. You understand that, I know. You read the news. You have the same fears.

During those years of growing up without her, when I needed my mother most, I developed a plan. The day he entered that penitentiary as a convicted prisoner, legally I changed my name. I earned a BA, and then an MA in Social Work. All the while I was doing time too, waiting for Mifflin.

In anticipation of his release, I changed my hair colour, even the colour of my eyes—I needed contact lenses anyway, and blue to green was not much of a stretch. The business suit and crisp haircut that had become my disguise were a far cry from the sweater and skirt and shoulder-length hair he would remember.

With my excellent grades at university, I could have taken a job anywhere, but I wanted to work for the province, in correctional services.

Normally the so-called easy cases—like Mifflin—are the plums and newbes are assigned the junk no one else wants. I told my supervisor I needed extra work and begged for Mifflin's case—I wanted to research a case with a good prospect for rehab. She was happy to get rid of an extra file folder.

The Thursday morning of his release—Thor's Day—I phoned his wife and told her not to bother taking the six-hundred-kilometre bus ride to the prison. "I'll get him," I assured her. I left a message with the warden's office with instructions for Mifflin to meet me at the gate; I would drive him home. It was partially true—I did meet him at the gate.

The day was overcast, I remember, with steely clouds hanging low over the British Columbia mountains, determined to imprison the sun. The day suited my mood. It's inappropriate to feel jolly when a life is about to be extinguished. Even I know that.

I watched him walk out of the prison a free man. Mifflin reeked of guilt. But his guilt would not bring back my mother—and I wasn't about to forgive him. He would not make it home to his lovely wife and three children. He would not resume his good works in the community. He wouldn't make it past the parking lot.

Mifflin hadn't seen me in six years—since the case finally came to trial. My testimony had been brief. Over that week as the travesty of justice unfolded, he faced front and didn't look at me, although my eyes were drawn to him like iron filings to a magnet. I will never forget his left profile.

He looked the same, although his muscles were more developed—presumably from working out in the prison gym—and his cheeks more gaunt.

"Mr. Mifflin," I said, removing my glove and extending a hand. I wanted to feel the skin of this killer, the flesh that held the knife that had ended my mother's life. Is the flesh of a killer different from normal flesh? Would I feel the slippery blood of my mother that had seeped into his pores ten years before, blood that could never be washed away?

He shook my hand. His grip was not as firm nor as cool as I'd anticipated, but mine made up for it. He looked at me skeptically. "Shelagh McNeil," I said, "your new case worker."

Mifflin ran a hand through his greying hair; his brown eyes reflected confusion; he didn't know what to do with me. Maybe it was hard for him to be in the presence of a woman without a weapon of destruction.

"I have a car," I said. "This way."

I slid behind the wheel of the tan Nissan and he got in on the passenger side. I sat without turning the key, staring at his left profile.

He fidgeted, punched his thigh in nervousness, looked out the window. "Mind if I smoke?" he asked, pulling out a pack of Rothmans.

"Yes I do," I said.

He slid the pack back inside his jacket submissively. The silence was getting to him.

Finally he turned. "Do you need my address?"

"I know your address."

He scratched his head. "Can we get going? My wife's waiting. Christmas, you know. The kids and all."

"I know everything I need to know about you, Mr. Mifflin. All but one thing."

He waited, expectant.

"How did you feel as you murdered Mrs. Brautigam."

"How did I feel?" Now he was really uncomfortable. "Look, I talked to a shrink about all this, inside." He shifted and turned away from me. "Can't we talk about this later?"

"That's not possible, Mr. Mifflin."

He turned back. His eyes narrowed. He struggled to make a connection but there wasn't enough left of the girl who had watched her mother die. And it wasn't just the physical changes. I was no longer vulnerable, but he was.

He put his hand on the door handle. "Look, I'll catch the bus."

"The last bus is gone," I told him, "and I believe your parole stipulates that you are required to meet certain conditions, including working with your social worker. I simply want to know how you felt, that's all. When you stabbed Mrs. Brautigam twenty-eight times, and her blood gushed out, splattering you with red gore, and her screams filled your ears. And her son and daughter watched their mother die. How did you feel?"

He turned away. In a small voice he said, "I don't remember."

"I need to know how it feels," I said, slipping a hand into my briefcase, "because I don't remember feelings either." I hit the automatic door lock.

His head snapped back.

I used both hands to plunge the knife into his left eye. I had sharpened the Henckel daily after the police returned it. Most of the six inches slid in as easily as if it were pie dough I was cutting. I felt the finely-honed steel pass the eyeball and enter the pale brain tissue. He clamped his hands around my wrists; I couldn't tell if he was trying to pull the blade out or helping me push it in as far as it would go, but I held tight.

Mifflin went rigid. He stared at me for a moment, his face creased with uncomprehending horror, his pierced brain struggled to make the awful connection. His hand clutched the handle and he yanked the blade out. Blood spurted into my face, across the windshield, over his brand new prison-release shirt. He was shocked. Before he could react, I grabbed the knife and stabbed him twenty-seven more times, counting aloud. He didn't struggle, like my mother. He did not possess her character. The same character her daughter possesses.

The media would be surprised to know how passionate I felt as I stabbed him. My feelings, the first after so many years, were surely different from whatever Mifflin must have felt as he murdered my mother, although I'll never be certain. Pressure lifted from my heart when I pierced his. My mind cleared of thoughts as blood and brain tissue gushed from his mutilated left eye. His body cooled and I defrosted. I watched his life dwindle much as I had watched my mother's life fade, and now I feel released. Finally I've reached the end of the corrupted vein and moved beyond that constricting tunnel into a world of complete and utter freedom. I have arrived back where I began, into a state of innocence. Justice has been accomplished. Don't you agree?

Many questions have been asked about me, but I have questions of my own and I hope you'll consider them calmly and rationally now that you've heard how it was. Do I deserve a worse fate than Mr. Mifflin's? Is my crime more heinous than his? I'm charged with murder one. The papers say I'll get life in prison unless I plead insanity, but I can't do that. He killed my mother. I killed him. What act could be more rational? An eye for an eye. Isn't that the purest form of justice? You decide.

Italics
by Fabrizio Napoleone

Fabrizio Napoleone grew up in Hamilton, Ontario, home of many well-known racketeers and gangsters, particularly Johnny Papalia and Rocco Perri, both of whom came to sudden, violent ends. A Web designer by profession, "Italics" is Fab's first published story, although another work, "Eight," was shortlisted for the 2003 CBC Literary Prize in the short fiction category. Currently, Fab is working on a short story collection.

It was the last time I would visit the Rail Street Tavern. Not that I didn't want to go back, but my uncle, *Zio* Paulie, had passed away a few weeks before and his tavern, a local institution in Hamilton's North End, had been sold. I was there to pay my respects.

In some Italian families custom has it that the oldest male inherits certain traditional tasks. This was the reason for my return. Entrusted to me was the duty of ensuring that the wishes of my late uncle were carried out as requested in his will; with his wife since passed, his two daughters were to receive the bulk of his estate. Zio Paulie, however, left a few little surprises. For this reason I had asked my cousin, Momo—the Sundance Kid to my Butch Cassidy—to meet me at the tavern that day.

The place had changed only slightly since I was last there some fifteen years before. It used to be a big part of my life, that narrow tavern where I bused tables and washed dishes after school, before I headed West to explore the world.

On quiet nights, and when my zio no longer required the assistance of the waitress, after the cook had closed the kitchen, he would manage the tavern with the help of only a busboy. Both Momo and I were given jobs at the tavern and, as personal favours to our mothers, given alternate shifts. A cunning move, I think, to keep us apart. We were less trouble that way.

As I looked around the empty tavern, the memories slowly seeped back. I easily imagined Zio Paulie with his white waist-apron appearing behind the bar. He had a stern and serious look about him, like the faces of the worn-out steelworkers that used to come in for drinks after their shifts.

The tables and chairs were stacked on top of each other, boxes piled high ready for the movers to take away. The jukebox was gone but the walls were the same: engraved white stucco with sculpted scenes of Venice and Pisa.

From inside one of the boxes, I pulled out an autographed photo of Angelo Mosca, the big defensive tackle for the Tiger-Cats from the '60s and '70s. Another photo, the Azzurri, circa 1982: the year Italy won the World Cup. It was here, in the Rail Street Tavern, that I watched that soccer finale with my uncle, a room full of football-fevered relatives and hookey-playing factory workers. On the walls were dusty outlines, now reminders of where those images had hung for so many years. Something was missing, however. I wasn't sure what.

I ran my hand along the edge of the wooden bar, rubbing it as if I were calling for my uncle's ghost to appear, maybe from out of the door in the floor, bringing up a case of beer or a few bottles of wine from the basement. Instead, it was the front door that opened. In came Momo and with him a little bit of the afternoon sun.

"Alessandro Delveccio," he announced. "It's about time you came home."

We greeted each other as familiar cousins do: with big hugs and giant smiles.

"It's good to be home," I said. "I missed this place."

"So, has it changed much?"

"Not much, really, but I did expect those four old guys in the corner to be still playing cards."

"The longest card game in the world? Just broke up a few weeks ago. They shut it down the day of Zio Paulie's funeral."

There was a pause, a moment of silence for our uncle. Nothing needed to be said.

"*Bicchierino*? Red wine—private stock?" said Momo. He stepped behind the bar, pulled out two glasses from one of the boxes and poured. "To the best boss two punks from Hamilton could ever ask for. *Salute*, to Uncle Paulie."

"*Salute* to Zio P.," I said and we raised our glasses and drank. "I'm glad we could hook up, Momo. Especially here. It's better this way. You know, appropriate."

"You couldn't make it to the funeral, eh? Still exploring the world?"

"Couldn't get back in time," I said.

"How long are you in town?"

"I've got business in Toronto on Monday then I head back." I reached inside my jacket and pulled out an envelope. "But, as executor of Zio Paulie's will, he left you a little 'something-something.' A little bonus for all those long hours you spent in here." I slid the envelope onto the counter.

Momo didn't touch the envelope. He just stared at it. "Zio P. was a real gentleman. A class act all the way," he said.

"Come on, open it. No strings," I replied. "All the nephews got the same. Nice little *boosta*, like it was your wedding or something."

Momo put the envelope in his pocket. "I'll open it later. Thanks, Alex," he said. "So, what's gonna happen to this place?"

"Been sold. Some *stuggats* from Toronto is going to make it into a bistro or something. Why didn't you take over, Mo? It was yours for the asking."

"Mine? You're the alpha male in the family. You're the smart one," he said taking a drink.

"Well, there's a difference between book smart and streetwise," I said. "I figure it worked out just about right."

"Yeah, and I'm not a bartender anyway. I got my own thing goin'. Got a couple partners. You remember Double G and Chooch?"

"Sure, I remember those guys. Is there potential for trouble? You know, I worry about you sometimes."

"No, I got everything under control. We don't step on anybody's toes and we don't get too greedy. It's just a sideline, ya know?"

I gave a nod of understanding. In Hamilton, you don't ask too many questions about another man's sidelines.

"Oh, one more thing," I said. "Specifically left to you by Zio Paulie. The lawyer says it's in the basement."

I went around the bar, lifted the door in the floor and descended the steep, old steps. Momo followed.

The pull chain for the light was at the bottom of the staircase. The bulb was dim but cast enough light on the now-empty shelves and wine racks. In that basement we had watched our fathers and uncles press grapes for their wine. This is where they smoked their proscuitto, and cured their homemade cheeses just like they did back in Abruzzo. And, I thought to myself, this is where those old customs will stay.

In the corner of the basement was a large trunk, narrow, almost coffin-shaped, most likely brought over from Italy when the families emigrated. My parents had a similar one in their basement. With that trunk they crossed the Atlantic, carrying all their worldly possessions and all their hopes.

"There it is," I said. "The trunk is all yours. It's in the will."

"What am I gonna do with that old thing?" said Momo.

"I don't know," I shrugged. "Maybe there's something inside."

We lifted the lid together. There was only one item in the trunk. It was a hockey stick. That's what was missing from the bar-room wall, the old hockey stick that used to hang under the television set like a rifle on a gun rack.

Momo was quiet. He lowered the lid and sat down on the trunk laying the stick across his lap. The stick was six feet of ash, old and hard, black tape still stuck to the blade's slight left-handed curve. It looked as if it had played a hundred hockey games. Momo ran his hands along the shaft, over the worn, stencilled letters and the indecipherable autograph.

Neither of us was certain of the stick's history. Its origin was fuzzy. We had always assumed one of the players from the city's junior teams had given it to our uncle.

"More sentimental value than anything else," I guessed.

"You know," Momo said looking me in the eye, "Zio P. hired us as a favour to our mas, keep us off the street, that sort of thing."

"I suspected as much," I said.

"Well, one night, I think I was about thirteen—you must have been fourteen already. I came in after school."

"And?" I said, taking a seat beside him.

"I was starting on the dishes, so I could see through the little waitress window, you know the serving hatch? That night the place had a few regulars and a few not-so-regulars. Sitting at the end of the bar was a fat man and his date. He had the kinda face like we would have seen him around, maybe at a wedding or something. But I didn't know his name, didn't know who he was. Zio was behind the bar, chatting him up. At the front table were those four old guys."

I could picture this easily since I had served those old men countless times as well, each with a half-filled glass of Chianti and a handful of Italian playing cards. The only other items on the table were an astray and *fiasco*—the straw-covered wine bottle, in constant need of refilling.

Momo continued with his story.

"Did ya forget that your job was to buss the tables?" asked Zio Paulie peering at Momo through the kitchen door. Momo dried his hands and walked over to the old men, picked up the empty *fiasco* and replaced the dirty ashtray with a clean one. As he did this, Momo glanced out the window. It was beginning to turn dusk. A man in a bad-fitting dark suit, not unlike the one the fat man at the bar wore, stood under the tavern's awning smoking a cigarette, watching passers-by and flicking the butts toward the worn railway tracks that cut the street in half.

One of the old men mumbled something to Momo. Momo took the empty bottle to the back of the bar.

"I think they want more wine," Momo said to his uncle.

"I'm already on it," said Zio Paulie, filling another bottle from the tap of the *damigiana* that sat behind the bar.

"Zio, what card game are they playing?" Momo asked.

"Those old guys? They was here when I open this place. They play same card game since I dunno when. It's so old they forgot da name," he smiled to himself.

"And, who's the guy standing out front?"

"You asking a lot of questions," said Zio Paulie. "He's nothing. You no worry about."

"Well, I can already guess he's something 'cause you're being so evasive."

"Evasive? What the hell kinda word is dat? You gonna be a college man like your cousin Alex?"

Momo didn't answer.

"Well, I guess you're gettin' old enough to know a few things. He's with that gentleman." Zio motioned toward the large man at the end of the bar.

"The fat guy?" Momo whispered.

"That is Mr. Carlo Ventura."

"That's Chuckie Cheese Ventura?"

His uncle scowled at him, as if he should know better. "Don't ever call him that unless you wanna lose some teeth. You understand? That guy, he no play around. I'm just pointing him out because it's better you know who's who, then going around not knowin' who's who. Understand?"

Momo nodded not taking his eyes off the fat man. His uncle pushed him back into the kitchen to finish the dishes.

Between the bar-room and the kitchen was the waitress window, where the cook would serve up the dishes. It was a good five feet off the floor, and we, in our early teens, would stand on tiptoe to peer through it. This is how Momo watched Mr. Carlo Ventura.

Carlo wasn't like the men that worked in the steel mills. He was huge, like the football players whose photographs hung on the wall. His hair was combed back, as if he just got back from the barber down the block. He wore a suit and a gold ring on his baby finger. The white-haired woman at his side did not look the wife type. The fat man leaned over and whispered in her ear. She giggled. He swished his glass and took a swig, swallowing the Scotch and crushing the ice with his teeth.

"Eh Paulie, another Scotch and rocks. And get her a whatever-the-hell-it-is with the little umbrella." Carlo turned to his date, "Put a quarter in that thing, will ya, Honey?" He motioned to the jukebox. "See if they got some Frankie or Dino."

Honey held out her hand as Carlo reached into his pocket for some change. He dropped a few coins in her palm. Honey strolled across the room toward the jukebox, but paused for a moment at the autographed hockey stick that hung on the wall under the television. As she stared at the illegible autograph she clicked the coins together in a steady rhythm.

Zio Paulie put the drinks down in front of Carlo.

"I guess you must be wondering what the frig I'm doin' here, hey Paulie? You thought you was rid of the fellas?"

"Carlo, nothing going on here. You know dis is neutral ground. I am clean," Zio said. "You are not supposed to shake me. You can ask the Old Man."

"Yeah, yeah, I know the deal ya got with him," said Carlo. "You paid your dues way back. You are Switzerland, my friend. I just came in here to reminisce a little, ya know?" Carlo took a drink. "The Old Man. What a laugh. He's in trouble, ya know. His heart is winding down. Yeah, he gets sick and so does my career. He's got me on a leash. After what I did for him. Look where he's got me now, a bag man for chrissakes." Carlo took another swallow. "I'm just blowin' off steam, Paulie. I got no problem here. Just needed to get out of familiar surroundings for a little while."

Carlo leaned back on his bar stool to see if his man was still out front of the tavern. He then turned to look for Honey who was staring at the photograph of Guy Lombardo that hung on the wall. She clicked the coins together, sounding like a tiny clock marking time.

Carlo continued his story in a hushed voice, neither man realizing Momo was eavesdropping as he pretended to keep busy shuffling back and forth between the kitchen and bar. "You know, I stopped going to confession the day it was legal for me to drink. I confess all my sins to the bartender. And you, my friend, are one of the last bartenders that I can talk to. Old school, ya know?" He raised his glass to Zio. "Have a drink with me will ya, Paulie?"

"I don't drink, Carlo."

"A bartender that don't drink, well what do ya know?" he shrugged. "Didn't the Old Man sponsor your 'migration here. You were born in the mother country, no?"

Zio Paulie nodded.

"You are a rare breed, Paulie, a rare breed indeed. You ain't involved and you ain't gonna open your mouth." Carlo took a drink. "I remember when the streetcars used to come by here. You could ride those things all around Hamilton for a nickel." Carlo turned to the white-haired woman, now pressing buttons on the jukebox. "Hey, Honey, how ya doing over there?"

"How about Johnny Mathis?" she said, spilling a little of her umbrella drink on the Wurlitzer.

"Johnny Mathis? Johnny Mathis is not Sinatra. Chrissakes, he's not even Italian. Keep looking." He turned back to Paulie, loosened his tie and leaned in a little. "You know how I made my bones?" Carlo didn't wait for Paulie to answer. "I had to take down one of my own men. Had to be done. Like a snake bite—you gotta carve out the poison with a sharp knife. Fast, ya know?"

Uncle Paulie poured another Scotch.

"A truck gets ripped off. Big truck, full of liquor. A good score, except for the fact that the guy that did it, he buys a brand new used car, a '71 Camaro, with cash money, just a couple of days after he gets rid of the booze. What a fuckin' *imbecile*."

"A few weeks after that, the Old Man puts two and two together and calls me in." Carlo took another drink. "Day before Christmas. These things are always near a holiday, symbolic like, you know? After that, they make me *martello della famiglia*." He gently pounded his fist on the bar. "That was a long time ago, Paulie, when the streetcars still came by here."

Carlo spotted Momo staring through the waitress window. Carlo gave him a who-the-hell-are-you look that almost made Momo piss his pants.

The jukebox lit up with the sounds of Count Basie. Honey walked over to Carlo, took him by the hand. Carlo slid off the bar stool and they started a clumsy dance in the middle of the room. The old men drank their wine and dealt another hand. At that moment, everyone was enjoying themselves. Just like the old days, imagined Momo, when the streetcars used to come by.

Sinatra crooned "I've Got You Under My Skin."

Outside the streetlights flickered on. A loud pop. Momo peaked through the waitress window. The old men at the card table paused. One of them peered out the front window and then turned back to look at Carlo.

Carlo smiled at Zio Paulie, "Probably one of them factory trucks backfirin', eh?"

The front door swung open wildly. A young man appeared in the doorway waving a gun. In his other hand he carried a black cloth bag. He spotted Carlo and pointed the gun at him.

"What do you want?" asked Carlo.

"I'm glad you asked, fat man. I'm gonna tell you before I kill you," said the gunman, a vein bulging from the side of his neck.

Sinatra stopped singing, Count Basie's orchestra finished playing and a cold silence filled the room.

"What happened to Gus?" asked Carlo.

"Gus is on medical leave at the moment," said the gunman. "Not much of a body guard, either." He turned to Zio Paulie, "You, get over by the front door. Slowly."

Zio Paulie walked around the bar, opened the front door and winced at the sight of Gus.

"Drag him inside. Lock the door," shouted the young man. "Do it now or I'll pop this fat fuck right here!"

Zio did as he was told. Gus was bleeding, but still breathing. He curled up into a fetal position near the wall.

"I got no problem with you, bartender. I just need to take care of some business," he said.

Momo watched his uncle, silent and calm.

The young man motioned for Paulie to get back behind the bar. He dropped the cloth bag and then glanced briefly at the old men. "You fellas keep playing," he ordered and they silently obliged.

Carlo glanced at the half-filled glass of Scotch and rocks that sat on the bar. He seized it and shattered it across the gunman's temple and with the broken tumbler still in his hand, Carlo shoved the jagged pieces toward the young man's face.

The young man pulled the trigger, twice. The first shot hit Carlo in the stomach. The second hit the wall near Honey. She fainted without a sound, resting under the stucco scene of Pisa.

Momo froze in the kitchen, his knuckles white gripping a dinner plate. The gunshots were still ringing in his ears as he thought about making a run for it out the back door, but his legs wouldn't move. He leaned slightly, to look out the kitchen door toward the bar. Zio Paulie, still safe behind the counter, remained calm, watching for the young man's next move.

Carlo was on the floor near his stool, holding his stomach, trying to stop the flow of blood from his big belly. "Who the fuck are you?" he said.

The young man stepped up close. "Who am I?" he said, wiping the blood from his face, "My name got changed a long time ago, Chuckie Cheese. It got changed the day you killed my father." The young man's face was crazed with a bloody smile. "Because of you, I got sent to Sudbury. Northern fuckin' Ontario. You know what's in Sudbury? Nothing, man. Nothing, but damn snow and cold."

"What are you talking about—I killed your father?" Carlo winced in pain.

Momo imagined Carlo going through all the unspeakable acts he had committed, trying to figure out which dead man the stranger referred to.

"I couldn't come back to this city because of you," said the young man as he pushed the muzzle of the gun into Carlo's cheek. "You kept me from being who I was supposed to be. You fucked with my destiny, fat man."

"You're crazy," said Carlo, spitting up blood.

"Crazy? Yeah, you would be too if you'd been breathing that Sudbury sulfur all these years."

Momo peeked through the waitress window. Honey was still passed out. Carlo squirmed on the floor, snot slowly dripping from his nose. Gus lay motionless near the front of the bar where the old men had checked their bets. They were waiting to see how this hand, dealt by the young stranger, would play itself out.

Zio Paulie broke the silence. "Drink?" he offered.

The gunman nodded and wiped the blood from his eyes. He glanced at the black bag he'd dropped on the floor. He downed the shot of Sambuca and Zio Paulie poured another. The young man drank again.

"Still don't know who I am, eh? Let me give you a hint. But it's gonna cost ya," he said as he booted Carlo under the chin and then motioned to Paulie for still another drink.

"Twelve years ago my father drove a Camaro."

Carlo's eyes widened.

"Nice one too, almost new," the gunman said. "They found it at the airport on Christmas Day. My father was in the trunk." He kicked Carlo in the stomach. "Happy fuckin' holidays. Do you know me yet?"

Carlo squirmed on the floor, collecting his strength.

"Your father stole and got caught. He knew the rules. He had it comin'."

"Yeah, I know he played outside the rules and he knew that too. But I've been doing some thinking and what gets me is, my old man, he was a truck driver, not a businessman. He couldn't have pulled off that trick all alone. There must have been someone else, know-what-I-mean? And my ma, who is still wearing black," he booted Carlo again and took another drink, "my ma tells me something. She tells me a twelve-year-old secret. See, you don't know my ma. My father had to tell her everything: who he was going with, how long he'd be—that sort of thing. You know how Italian women are."

Zio Paulie nodded. So did the old men at the card table.

"And the Camaro. My ma didn't know what happened to it until it showed up a few weeks ago, just after my eighteenth. Out of nowhere, it appears in my ma's driveway. When she saw that, she called for me to come back to Hamilton."

"The Old Man," mumbled Carlo, realizing only he could have arranged such a thing.

"That car used to be beautiful. Still is with the nice rims, chrome radio," continued the young man, "except for the smashed driver-side window." He kicked Carlo again.

"You and my father ripped off that truck. And when the Old Man started to ask questions, you whacked my father and let his reputation take the blame. Am I right?" Carlo did not answer. "Chuckie Cheese, I asked you a question. Am I right?"

Carlo tried to lift himself off the floor. "Don't call me that, you *stronzo*," he said, spitting blood.

The young man booted Carlo again and then reached for the cloth bag. He unzipped it and pulled out a chrome steering wheel with a large Camaro logo in the centre. He placed it around Carlo's neck like an Olympic medal and then put the muzzle of the gun into the fat man's mouth. Carlo's eyes crossed.

Momo looked away nervously. So nervous he dropped the dinner plate he'd been holding.

The young man stood up, pointed the gun at Zio Paulie. "What was that?"

"Justa the kid in the kitchen. He's the dishwasher. He's a little slow," said Zio Paulie. He had shifted to the end of the bar, now standing under the television.

The young man, his back to Zio Paulie, took a hesitant step toward the waitress window. He and Momo locked eyes.

In one fluid motion Uncle Paulie pulled the hockey stick from the wall and swung it, hard, like a Reggie Jackson home run swing. The young man's body whipped across the room and smacked against the jukebox. He was dead, thought Momo, or very unconscious.

The old men gathered up the cards, put their chairs on the table and proceeded out the back door. Momo still hadn't moved.

Zio Paulie took the phone from under the bar and made a call. Some men showed up. Men Momo had never seen before. They were not police. No one spoke as they cleaned up the tavern. As the last stranger was about to leave Zio Paulie had a hushed conversation with him. The man nodded, "I'll tell the Old Man," he said and he walked out the back.

In the kitchen, Zio Paulie said to his nephew, "You didn't see nothing, right, Momo? Your mother would kill me if she found out what happened here."

Momo nodded.

This was the story that Momo told me as we sat in the basement of the Rail Street Tavern; the last time either of us would set foot in the place.

"Momo, you didn't tell anyone? All these years?"

He shook his head. "Just you. It was like a dream I was supposed to forget."

We were silent for a while, sitting on that old trunk.

"You know the funny thing," Momo added. "We never saw Zio Paulie raise a glass, ever. But that night, after everyone else was gone, he poured himself a glass of wine."

Green Ghetto
by Vern Smith

Vern Smith grew up in Windsor, Ontario, about twenty-five minutes from the real green ghetto. He also grew up admiring the hard-edged writers of the Detroit pulp scene. Now resident in Toronto, Vern is a crime and political reporter, author of the short story collection *Glue for Breakfast*, and editor of the Western fiction zine *Kerosene Road*. He has contributed dark tales to the anthologies *Iced* and *Hard Boiled Love*. His story "The Gimmick" from *Hard Boiled Love* was a finalist for the 2003 Arthur Ellis Award for Best Short Story. And he is a regular contributor to *Canadian Screenwriter* magazine.

Mitchell Hosowich was pleased as a puppy with two tails and didn't think he had the right. Ever since he started growing this here wacky-tobaccy shit, he'd been thinking maybe it was time to skedaddle, show a speck of maturity.

Still, touring his leaning barn—newish boards mixed with original red—he couldn't help but breathe deeply through his nose, so musky it burned. Thinking, no sir, not even that so-called comedian was going to slip a cow patty in today's coffee tin. All week, Sadao Saffron had been peskier than a real job, phoning. Bring more, Mitchell.

Then, last night's message said some swingers yonder downtown at the Gentlemen's Choice Burlesque done beat him after he asks the cougar, Is that your son? And to the stud, Are you the guy videotaped himself rodeoing your best friend's wife in the movies? The rest was static, but they did what to his butt?

"The hell's my bible?" Mitchell said, feeling his back pockets, fronts. Locating a pack of Blunts in his faded mustard shirt, he removed a sheet, pinching a sticky bud, rolling a nice fatty, lighting, inhaling, thinking of how things used to be.

Way back when, Mitchell didn't know pot from a donkey's dong, only that he was a young man bent on being the lone hand on his own land. After getting a little cash together, maybe he'd figure out how to put the land to use, legally. Maybe, but whenever Mitchell came around to that kind of thinking, he'd ask himself what came first, grants or farmers?

Besides, if there'd been a good thing about the great American rust-out, it was that this part of Detroit had gone rural again, wild. As one scribe so eloquently wrote, it had long ago reverted to prairie so lush that

Natural Resources made a practice of exporting pheasants to improve the local gene pool. To Mitchell that was poetry, for pockets of wild turkeys and wilder dogs roamed amid the rabbits, geese and the odd coyote.

Mitchell couldn't reckon how they all found their way, but shit, left to its own devices, most everything was overgrown with trees, vines, weeds, and all sorts of wild flowers. So much so bureaucrats even came up with a highfalutin' name for it over cheese sandwiches.

"The green ghetto," Mitchell said quietly.

Pruning as he smoked, putting some baggies together, he remembered the archives left in the basement—claims that a rock formation near the southeast corner of his land had been the site of some skirmish, circa 1812. Mitchell didn't bother verifying that. To him, it was just another safe place to grow fairly good Detroit dope—a Midwest Stonehenge dismissed as insignificant.

Moseying on in from the Polish suburb of Hamtramck, Mitchell had struck his claim back in '74, the year Coleman Young became mayor. Same year seven hundred and fourteen slickers went to the big bone yard. Got so bad at one point, Coleman told criminals to hit the white side of Eight Mile Road. So yeah, pale face was on the run, Coleman left behind to sell off the badlands for overdue taxes, or a portion thereof.

Last farmer to actually work the land, name of Fryer, sold out to speculators, who lost their Levi's after the riots in '67. Mitchell, in turn, snapped up his two dozen acres for thirty-six hundred dollars and change. As part of the package, he had himself a couple barns, a farmhouse, and a pasture—all salvageable with a bit of elbow oil.

Every summer, he paid some local kids to set up shop for a few weeks on the I-75, selling tomatoes and corn that served as camouflage. Leftovers went to food co-ops, so right there, he had a downright respectable front. But yonder downtown, a new ballpark was named after a bank, the football field a car company. Folks were patronizing the casinos, along with little boutiques and eateries that had been springing up. Slowly, people were coming back, and Mitchell couldn't reckon how much longer he'd be allowed to go on like this.

Catori Jacobs chose a stars-and-stripes bikini for the first anniversary of September eleventh, figuring gynecology row would see it as patriotic. Kind of like Jewel singing "God Bless America" during the seventh-inning stretch, tits half out of something between a flag and a tank top.

Pulling up hemmed denim short-shorts, doing the button fly, she reached for thigh-high stretch-leathers with tie-dyed stitching, working her nines in, kneeling on the bed to get a good look a herself in the mirror.

The lopsided part in her coarse hair framed caramel freckles in an upside down V. Above her hips, a belt with jade details rode too high, so she loosened it. Sliding into the buckskin car coat, feeling for the last baggies—she didn't like taking dope downstairs *in*to the Motown Hoedown any more than she liked leaving it up here in her roomette above the place. It's just that girls could get competitive and there'd been stories, most notably about that stripper with the Brazilian—Danny Zalev, the owner, called her the Mohawk Pussy—dousing Tabasco on the electronic bull back in May. Freakin' strip joint with an electronic bull on stage—like what part of Detroit had that Hosowich said this was? Freakin' farmer's ghetto, something like that?

Anyway, while two girls were off on a scare to the free clinic after unknowingly sitting in ass-kick sauce, someone broke into their roomettes upstairs lockers. Mohawk Pussy denied all, but Catori was thinking, Someone ransacked something, when her two-forty knocked early.

"It's Ronnie."

Catori removed two eighths from a zippered seam, undid the lock on her roomette door. Ronnie—Veronica Cake, she called herself—let herself in, locked up, reaching into a tiny purse, extending two twenties, a five.

Taking the money, Catori checked out what Veronica did to those poor Wranglers. Six inches of material cut from the thighs, save the seams—presto: denim garters. And yes, she was wearing a handkerchief as a halter, classy.

"Also," Veronica said, "I want to buy for a friend, can we catch up?"

"If I still have some."

"No—first time, in what, five, seven weeks? It's like everyone's going dry." Veronica brushed her curled bang, revealing a second eye—she *did* have two—white liner. "May as well be back in Wichita. That's where I'm from by the way, you?"

Catori adjusted a suede five-gallon in the mirror, careful not to do that thing. But dammit, she was biting her lip anyway. "Death Valley."

"C'mon."

"Better than Detroit, warm, plus we have a national park. Detroit have a national park?"

Veronica thought all Death Valley had was the park, but didn't mention it on the way out.

Feeling one last time for the baggies in her car coat, Catori left almost three minutes into Dwight Yoakam's song. Locking up, tilting her head down the stairs, singing along with "Suspicious Minds," thinking how she preferred the Fine Young Cannibals' take. Preferred it? It was the best freakin' cover in the history of covers. The video didn't hurt either, Roland Gift glittering, shaming Elvis.

Dwight faded as she opened the gunmetal door, seeing Mohawk Pussy down on one knee, pushing herself up. Good timing: R.J. the DJ reminding all five patrons she's available, two-for-one dances until four. Now put your hands together for the Gorgeous Gina DiCicco.

Gina freakin' DiCicco—Hosowich swore she was Eye-talian too. Close enough to olive, anyway, and no offence, but it was probably best to take herself a stage name of Gina in a bucket of blood like this.

Bucket of blood—she'd lived in ratfuck Ontario for thirty-seven years and couldn't remember a freakin' Polack cowboy yet. Now here she's working for one, trying to be so damn PC after he says, Make like yer Eye-talian—and what had he called her? Oh yeah, a First Person of Canada, like a CBC documentary or something.

Cher was singing "Halfbreed," little inside joke to keep Catori sane, as she walked onstage hearing that elder in her head, saying maybe she had too much cream in her coffee for a card. Then, from the front row, the here and now.

"If there's a good thing came out of all this trouble, it's that everyone—and I mean everyone—is a comin' together," the one called Cooley said. "Look at her. She knows what day it is."

"An American girl," said Mickey Joseph, owner and operator of the nearby Mickey Joseph Service Station. His prices were higher by reason there wasn't a drop of gas for fourteen minutes either way. "One with a whiskey-stained soul, but an American girl nonetheless—you can tell."

Placing a folded towel on the electronic bull, mounting, Catori rocked slowly in first gear, watching Veronica through ferns near the back—hooking thumbs into loops, working the Wrangler garters down for some swinger lady. Apparently there was a roving club for that sort of thing around here. Clove and Butternut, the lifestyle people in these parts called it.

Mitchell reached into the stall to stroke his horse's snout. When the filly twitched, took a nip, he pulled back saying how he'd saved her, cared for her, even though she wouldn't be mounted.

"And goddammit, Hasty Kiss. That's why I got you in the first place, to ride you."

Twitching when Mitchell reached for her snout again, taking another nip, he said to hell with her, figuring he might still catch that Indian girl's act. Watch her do that thing with the tattoo on her butt, one word at a time. Make sure everything was keno with Danny Zalev too. The hell'd Danny been anyway?

Zipping a dozen baggies into inside seams, he slid into his own buckskin coat, part of his system.

"Take care of your people, they'll take care of you," he always said.

Sadao, seven strippers and a drag-queen bingo caller were his newly minted Sandinistas—every one of them in buckskin. Mitchell'd swung a bulk deal with a nice Polish sweatshop back home that had been stuck on an order by the aforementioned disbanded gangbangers, saved some money. Whatever their demise, Mitchell couldn't see what a Nicaraguan political party tossed out by the CIA had to do with local drive-bys.

Dragging his spurs up the gravel drive—yeah, he liked his diggers as much as he liked saving—he heard the chickens squawking, made a mental note to buy more feed before the weekend. Climbing into the Ram van, hitting the ignition, 99.5 WYCD on the box. "Detroit's best country station," the DJ said, bringing up Johnny Cash, "The Beast in Me."

"Also Detroit's only country station," Mitchell shot back, following the curves of his long driveway.

He turned left, south on what used to be known as Medland, passing the sign that said Unassumed Road. Careful to drive at no more than fifty, he figured Mickey Joseph's Service Station to be a mile from home, no one minding the shop. Two miles from home, the marker was a boarded-up bodega: Smeetons. Another half-mile, and something that looked like creeping charlie ran in an angry weave over a box of a building. ZAKOR'S PRODUCE was faintly stencilled out front, mellow-yellow dandelions leading up to that cardboard sign again.

IF YOU THINK IT'S DRY NOW,
WAIT TILL NOVEMBER.

Mitchell slowed, eyeballing the rear-view. Alone, he veered onto the sidewalk, gave the gas a nudge.

From the Motown Hoedown's stage, Catori watched an aging frat boy join Veronica and Mrs. Robinson in the shrubbery, hearing the Clash, R.J. getting it right for a change—first song, side B, "The Guns of Brixton." Topper Headon singing, almost talking, asking when they kick down your door, are your hands going to be held high or fingering your gun?

Sliding the buckskin down her back, she closed her eyes, deciding at least there was one good thing about dancing here. By law, girls could *not* take their panties off, and who wanted to shave that thing every day anyway? Razor burn, she was thinking when the bullwhip bit hard.

It coiled around her neck, tight. One hand at her throat, other hanging onto saddle, wide-eyed, she saw the blurry image of someone scuffling with R.J. in the booth, punching her ride into overdrive.

"Got her in fifth already. Look at her, fighting like a silver bass," Cooley observed.

"Been around animals," said Mickey Joseph. "You can tell."

They groaned when she was tossed—her five-gallon rolling sideways, nipples peeking over the stars and stripes. Looking up, she saw the one with the tight face up close—smiling, pulling hand over hand.

"DEA," Enid Bruckner said, reeling Catori to the edge of the stage, yanking her over. "Now let's see if we're holding any D on our person."

Catori awkwardly landed on her feet, stumbling, standing upright. "You're going to strip-search a stripper?"

Hand on her hip, Enid pointed, down.

"You couldn't just wait a few freakin' songs?"

"Your pants, I said."

Catori scrunched her face to one side, undoing buttons, shaking hot pants down to her boots. "Ever wish you did more experimenting back at the academy?" One foot stepped out, the other kicking denim to Enid, who was still pointing, down. Catori looked at herself, patriotic panties. "Supposed to have at least this much on at all times, the law."

"Then how come you're wearing tearaways?" Enid turned sideways. "Fowler, a little help, please."

"What?"

Enid looked at Fowler Stevens, pointing her head. "Subdue the suspect."

He looked at Catori. "Why?"

"To intimidate her."

Holding his hands up like a doctor, sterile, he awkwardly took Catori's shoulders, turning her, pushing her against the short stage wall. Enid stepped back, reading the tattoo on Catori's buttocks—one word on the left, another on the right—leaning in, breathing Hennessy. "I hear from a funny man downtown you're selling." Sliding her hand down, pinching one of the words. "*In* the Hoedown."

"Only thing I'm selling you're holding."

Enid looked to Fowler. "Find anything in her coat?"

"Clean as a gated community, same as her room."

"Take it anyway—evidence."

"*Of what?*"

"Evidence that Sadao Saffron had the same coat, custom job, same label: Sandinistas. Plus he had eyes like Robert Downey Jr.'s mugshot. Yet somehow he's also clean." She looked at Mickey Joseph, four others, counting. "Fowler's gonna take all five of you to the pool room for drinks, unofficial briefing for your peace of mind."

Fowler looked concerned, money.

"Agency plastic." Enid looked back at Mohawk Pussy—tan vest open, silver dollar nipples. "Take the help with, and ask for gloves—we're out."

Passing a run-over prairie dog, poor thing, Mitchell sparked up at the top of the news—Linda Lee reporting a bust on gangs of marijuana bandits shipping Canadian pot into Detroit.

Counter-clockwising the volume when she got to the part about possible links to al Quaeda, Mitchell allowed for the possibility that paranoia was in the mix. Same time, he'd cut back to fifty-nine plants this year. Worst case, sixty seemed like too damn many. Like at sixty he was definitely financing some sort of religious commies gonna blow up the Detroit–Windsor tunnel. Luckily, the African Violet Mix made up the difference.

He'd started a dozen plants on the concoction after reading a *High Times* article. Seeing instant results, all his Marys got a helping, another in August. Would have given them more, but last time the kid at Gall's Hardware—Tyler's young son, name of Ivan—was working the cash, pointing at one of the twenty bags, asking did Mitchell have African Violets? No, he referred to the part about "other flowering plants"—he had Portulacas, young man, a lot of Portulacas.

More trouble than it's worth, Mitchell decided, thinking about something else, anything. That Indian girl, for instance, she came over to work the Hoedown for him as a favour to Phil Legace, who ran a slightly larger racket in Dresden, Ontario near Catori's reservation. What was it? Tadpole Island? No, it was Walpole. Whatever, Mitchell had looked her name up, and in fact it was *not* Eye-talian—a Native Web site saying she's happiest expressing herself creatively.

Hehehe, Legace said she had trouble—something about lassoing a young RCMP narco copping free feels, hog-tying him—which was why she was here in the first place: hiding. The important thing was that she was clearing a good two-grand a week, and business was business no matter what that tattoo on her backside said.

"LUCKY YOU." Enid snapped a pair of yellow gloves, snug. "Still say you're not selling?"

"My ass is so clean you can eat it, lady."

Enid spit on her middle finger. "All you need to do is take me to *your* dealer—the source." Catori laughed when the moist latex touched her. "Something funny, Gina?"

Catori looked over her shoulder at the woman's thin fingers. "You got anything bigger?" She waited for a reaction, but the old broad just smiled, sides of her face pulling, nose disappearing in too many auburn highlights.

Mitchell tossed the roach, looking in the rear-view, bloodlines in his grey-blues. Feeling a bit warm—that Mal Sillars of News Four said Indian Summer was *done*, the devil—he fought out of his buckskin as he pulled into the Motown Hoedown. Parking spots everywhere. A woman walked in front of him.

Too old for a dancer, he thought, reaching to the sunflap for his aviator glasses. Looking back at her through mirrored frames, she had fine, child-bearing hind-parts, flaring at that tight ankle skirt, clay stitching. Plus she had to be five-ten in shit-kickers, substantial, and Mitchell liked big girls because they worked harder. But what was with her face? Like a girl that age had to moisturize. And whoa Nelly, what kind of badge was she flashing?

Enid Bruckner, DEA
Special Agent, Michigan

"Just courting to the Hoedown for some bark juice, ma'am," Mitchell said.

"No courting just yet, cowboy."

Mitchell pushed his hat back, shucks. "You flirting with me?"

"Crime scene." Looking at his white straw stetson, blue feather. "Maybe terrorism."

Mitchell stroked his horseshoe moustache. "Pardon?"

"Sick new form of lashing out at Yankee decadence. A lot of chatter, FBI says, electronic, then zap—A-rab-looking man whips a ballerina wears the flag as a bra, Anti-American."

Seeing the younger detective walk out carrying Catori's coat and a bull-whip, Mitchell resisted the urge to look down at his own buckskin, chatting up the DEA lady instead. "Sure someone's not stringing you a whizzer?"

"You saying I'm being pissed on?"

Catori carried two Farmer Jack grocery bags, walking out in jeans tucked into her boots. Up top, her torso was draped in a blue poncho with a crested brown horse. Mitchell passed her with a couple more Jack sacks, opening the passenger side. Rounding the van, he scanned the lot, clear, jumping in, keying the ignition. "Now, I am sorry." Throwing it into reverse, backing out. "But *somebody's* stringing me a whizzer."

"For the last time, it wasn't the freakin' Arabs."

Punching it into drive, he pulled out, turning north on Unassumed Road, saying he'd see that she got out of dodge with some greenbacks, but was she sure?

"It was the DEA woman, the one with the tight face. Like I'd just sold some to Veronica Cake, she calls herself."

"One wears so much powder she can't blush?"

"You're thinking of Mohawk Pussy. Veronica's supposed to look like Veronica *Lake*—actress with the peek-a-boo bang."

Mitchell held a hand over half his face. "One-eyed hairdo?"

Catori managed a smile, a nod. "Ever since Kim Basinger did her in *L.A. Confidential*, every club has to have one. Anyway, she's dancing for the DEA woman when I close my eyes. Then there's a snap, whip around my neck. Bitch drags me to the front of the stage. Then the young one, Fowler—looks like the guy from *Sex, Lies, and Videotape*—he holds me down while she says, Take me to your dealer—you—then checks me for— she calls it—keister stash."

That seemed to interest Mitchell, his stache stirring. "Sadao Saffron did say *something* about his butt, but there was static."

"Yeah." Catori nodded. "DEA woman said she did the same thing to him last night—stoned, but clean. Also said he had the same coat, told them about me. You know him?"

Parked, leaning out the window, Fowler watched the colourful bird strutting across Unassumed Road. "You're telling me this's still Detroit proper?"

"That's right," Enid said, propping the handwritten sign up.

Fowler pointed at the bird. "Then what the shit is that?"

Enid, taping the sign's broken wood legs together, said, "Male."

"I know what it is. I mean, what the shit is it doing in the city?"

"This here is what they call a green ghetto. Means the urban ecosystem is all fucked up." Enid fished the hammer out of her tool box, gently tapping the sign back into the ground. "You know everyone left after the riots, half anyway. Here in particular the land was being developed, but all they ended up doing was levelling. Now everything's overgrown. Birds fly over thinking they must've hit Iowa early—Canadian geese, wild turkeys."

"So, Unassumed Road, that's supposed to be funny, some kind of local joke?"

Enid opened the driver side. "Means the city doesn't service it anymore—drive at your own risk."

"Huh." As she dumped her tool box on the back-seat floor, Fowler read the sign. "'If you think it's dry now...' This yours?"

Enid nodded, hitting the ignition. "Getting the natives running scared, rattled."

"It's the goddamn prairie—the hell's gonna read it?"

"Someone's rattled. Who else would run this over but a drug criminal? Who would *care*? Think of it as bait."

Fowler watched Enid wipe her mouth with a red paisley hanky, guiding the stardust-grey Bronco north, heading for I-75. All right, she was supposed to break him in. Fine, he was in fresh from the Baltimore drug squad, so what the shit did he know about the urban prairie? But she wasn't supposed to use dish gloves, and that much about DEA work he already knew. Then again, what the shit was he supposed to say?

"Where to now?"

"Menjo's," Enid said. "Girly-man bar on West McNicholes."

He checked his Casio digital, three thirty-four, early.

"Drag queen runs afternoon bingo," she said, "also selling."

"And we know this how?"

"Kendra."

"Kendra?"

"Kendra Mann, runner-up Miss Empress Michigan."

Fowler nodded, satisfied. "Another reliable source."

Enid let that go, said, "The winner runs the bingo like territory. Same thing with the comedian at the burlesque, the dago peeler from the Motown Hoedown—common thread being they sell while doing gigs that don't pay, at least not enough. Gig's a front."

"Due respect." Fowler raised a hand. "Common thread seems none of them happen to be holding a girl named Mary."

"Doesn't matter. Soon as we find one, we have something to scare them with, get the supplier—the grail."

"Grail?" Now what was she talking about?

"The link, Fowler." She rolled a hand. "Between terror and drugs in Michigan."

"Link—what did that cowboy say again? 'Sure someone's not stringing you a fizzer?'"

"I'm telling you, these people call themselves the Sandinistas. Says so inside their coats, behind the collar."

Fowler wrinkled his nose, showed teeth. "So now we're on the lookout for thought-provoking Nicaraguans?"

"Sandinistas means political." Enid pulled a small pad of paper from the dash, motioning to the laptop between them. "And something makes me like that cowboy. Run his plates."

"But he didn't have a coat, why him?"

"Found navy paint on my sign, could be same as his van."

Fowler watched as she went for the red-paisley hanky, wiping her mouth again. "Hey, can I ask did you get that from Veronica Cake?"

Mitchell steered high, trying to smile, natural. "Federales must have Danny's balls on a skillet. He's set it so I could have a girl selling out of the Hoedown going on fourteen of sixteen years. Only exceptions being '88, locusts, and '94, the first chopper program. I pulled everything a bit premature that year, dumped it on Legace. Very next week, some slicker in Inkster shoots the chopper down with a varmint gun."

"Varmint gun," Catori said. "What about Danny Zalev? He say anything?"

"No." Mitchell licked his lips. "But then he didn't check in either."

"Danny's MIA, a dealer's gloved—how about a heads-up, huh?"

"I told you—static."

"Static." Her gold-brown eyes narrowed to bulls' eyes. "You told Legace I'd be safer than an ox on a hobby farm."

"Okay, okay."

"Take care of your people—you left me twisting in the wind, man. Like, *you* exposed *me* to DEA."

"All right already."

"Don't you 'all right already' me. You got DEA up the ass, a dealer's gloved, and you don't think maybe you can drop a little warning my way? Legace'll slit your throat he hears this. *I'll* slit your—"

"Look." Mitchell briefly took his hands off the wheel, framing a gap between his front teeth, gold chopper below. "I thought Sadao got it over something he said. Talking about some guy gets caught taping sex he has with his best friend's wife in the movies, what's that supposed to mean?"

"The one she calls Fowler, I told you." Catori reached back, raising her ass, pulling a cassette from her pocket. "Looks like James Spader, the actor—he gets it on with Andie MacDowell, an unfulfilled housewife."

"I know *now*." Mitchell watched his eyes, quick in the sideview. "Danny, he been around?"

"Haven't seen him from Thursday." She slid the tape into his player, hit play. The Clash again, Topper Headon saying how this Greater London outlaw feels like Ivan, born under the Brixton sun.

"Okay, okay," Mitchell said. Thinking of that young kid hassling him over the African Violet Mix at Gall's Hardware, also name of Ivan, cutting the music.

"What?"

"Sounds a bit negatory just now. Also sounds like we got a hair in the butter." He hesitated, slowing down at the dandelion patch when he saw the sign already repaired. She leaned across his lap smelling like lemon thyme, putting an arm around him for balance, reading.

IF YOU THINK IT'S DRY NOW,
WAIT TIL NOVEMBER.

"The fuck?" she said. "You mean to tell me there was a sign on the road and you still didn't say anything? If you think it's dry—what the fuck is that?"

"Means we got to belly through the bush."

"You're not bellying through my bush, old-timer."

Mitchell accelerated, clenching teeth. "Means it's time to make ourselves scarce. Federales involved, dirty, right off her mental reservation."

"Hey."

"Let's just say it political correct—we got to go."

"Where?"

"Depends. All I know is I've got a lot of dope to unload, no time."

"You willing to cross the border?"

"Same thing I was thinking."

Then they both said Legace.

Mitchell nodded as they drove by his pasture, his shepherds, Wolfie and Lou, play fighting on a bale of hay. Simmi was chewing something, giving the familiar van a lazy moo.

"Okay, now what is *that*?" Catori said.

"Simmi. Simmental-Hereford cross."

She looked up and down the road. "You got power lines? Bad water?"

"No, why?"

"Why? Something's growing out of her freakin' head."

"Third horn, ten inches, almost."

Catori sighed, looking at the two-tone cow. "Same kind of things where I'm from—downstream from chemical valley—birth defects."

"Simmi's natural. Uncommon—like the cow patty on John Boy's face—but natural nonetheless."

"Why didn't you cut it off? That's what you're supposed to do to girl cows anyway."

"She's beautiful," Mitchell said, "as God intended."

Here we go. Catori motioned to the outhouse. Did he rent? Mitchell shook his head, uh-uh, turning into his drive, passing at a sign drenched in ivy.

MITCHELL P. HOSOWICH FARMS

"I'm the big sugar here." He put the van into park. "And that there outhouse is just for show, historical. Running water inside."

Catori followed him up the walk, saying, "You ever thought of being a real farmer, legit?"

"No."

"Why not?"

"What came first, young lady, grants or farmers?"

She didn't bother, nodding to his horse on the far side of the pasture. "Mind if I take her for a spin."

"A spin." He rounded a hammock hanging across the porch, keying the knob. "She's just to look at, Hasty Kiss." Whirling an index around his temple. "Loco."

"You some mail-order cowboy, can't break a horse?"

Ignoring that, he took his boots off at the landing. She did likewise, saying, "Why get a picture framed with your eyes closed?"

Mitchell turned to the frame on the wash stand. "That there's the last known picture of Little Dick West, and he's dead."

"He the one who died in shame after a botched train job? Got a hundred dollars or something."

"Common misconception," Mitchell said. "Time came where the law caught up with Little Dick, shot him. No shame. And it was more like three hundred dollars, big money in 1898."

Whatever, saying they had the same moustache, she followed him into the living room—an antique scale on a shelf, Little Dick West display plates, Tetley-Tea animals, old jeans everywhere—one pair on the faux cowhide loveseat, two more strewn over the Singer. "You sew?"

"Buy my range clothes used, mend them." Hitching his jeans, off-colour patch above the knee. "These here're Tommy's. I get most everything by the pound." Taking off his Stetson, showing her the inside rim, gold lettering, CALGARY CONVENTION & VISTOR'S BUREAU.

She had to admit he had a good smile when he got to talking about saving. But his hair was all over the place—freakin' missing link—and nice stache. Like was Little Dick West his guy or something?

Watching him walk to the phone, she asked why he had an answering machine? He looked at her, saying to take messages. No, she meant why didn't he have voicemail? He pointed at the tan button phone, saying he didn't want Michigan Bell to have copies of said messages.

Mail-order cowboy, huh—did she know how many times men outnumbered women on the prairie? Eight to one, thereabouts, she said, why? Drawing his chin to his chest, he recalled a time when a cowboy *had* to sew—stitches, hems, whatever.

There, he thought, hitting play, hearing his dancer at the Booby Trap speak of gloves. Next, his girl from the Black Orchid uttered the words keister stash. Neither was charged, but both had gone into hiding, their buckskins seized. What were they supposed to do, Mitchell?

He hit erase as the phone rang again. "Envy," he said, reading call display.

"Stripper?"

"No, drag queen calls bingo." Picking up, he said, "Hail the empress." Another string of words from another freaked-out dealer.

Envy said they were going to check her man too, only he took off because he really did have something in his ass, Envy's diamond. What kind of man was that anyway?

Mitchell waited until it was over, said, "Did they find anything on you?"

"She don't find the secret compartments. But she take my buckskin, gonna find like seven baggies. You got trouble, Hosowich?"

"Never mind. You got a stage out?"

"Stage—I run from the stage, you idiot. That is where the one with the tight face finds me—the stage."

"I mean transportation."

Envy paused. "Jes, I have my man's keys, his Firefly."
"Then get in and drive."
"Where?"
"Far away, and not now, but right now."
When Mitchell hung up, he looked into Catori's glare.
She said, "Now I don't feel so bad."
"Why?"
"Looks like you left all of us twisting."
Mitchell counted his fingers out, saying no, there were three more left. Catori looked at him wide-eyed, said, "Well?"
"Well what?"
"Aren't you going to call them?"

Mitchell thought how he'd rather be trolling thrift shops for funky cowboy gear, a better hat. But hush puppies, after he managed to get to two of girls, he was on the phone *again*. Telling Phil Legace he had a hair in the butter.

"Hypothetical, Phil. If I was to bet on the 59ers, what would an establishment yonder in Canada pay?"

Legace thought back how it was the 76ers in '94—code. "It's a good team, like last time?"

"Ever introduce Mary to Violet?" Mitchell said.

"I've heard good things. Okay, five days it will take, maybe five weeks, but can do. Same terms as with the 76ers, per 59er, indexed for inflation."

"Favourably?"

"Favourably—just get your team on the bus."

"Okay, see you in a few hours, Phil."

A few hours? That was fast. Legace said it sounded like two hairs in the butter. Hello, was Mitchell still there? It was supposed to be funny—two hairs. Yeah, Mitchell said, sorry to be a pill, Phil, but let's just say this ain't no hootenanny. And yes, Catori is cuter than a 'lil red truck. See you, bye.

Hanging up, he watched her close the fridge, holding a bag of Uncle Herschel's Soya Jerky. Looking at him hard again, then down at his Endangered Species belt buckle—The Giant Panda—she asked did that come with a tax receipt?

"I got one rule." He looked down at his stocking feet. "No critter-eatin' in this house."

"Telling me you're a vegan farmer?"

"Slaughtering ain't necessary for survival. Besides, didn't your people tell of when the land was lived on only by talking critters? Thought first persons are supposed to treat the land, water, and critters with respect, always. Especially critters—you got to learn to treat critters as your fellows, talk to 'em as such."

Catori nodded, Patience, white man, telling her what it is to be Native. "We don't hunt for sport. When we do, we use the whole animal, not just the meat. See, there's nothing wrong with the *eating*. It's the wasting, like cutting off sharks' fins, throwing the rest back—the disrespect."

"Yeah, well I bet the poor little tasties feel slightly dissed on the way down your gullet."

She pointed at his London calf leathers near the door. "You wear 'em."

"Used is okay." Tugging at his kangaroo belt. "Already dead, means I'm not creating demand, recycling. Now tonight, we're on with Legace."

She crossed the room, sitting in the middle of the loveseat, open palms on each cushion. "Got a plan?"

"Think so." He picked up the Sports, folding the page. "Jr. Red Wings playing the Spitfires at Joe Louis, pre-season game. I say we cross over with the hockey crowd, blend. Lotta people in Windsor love those Spits."

All right, she waited for the rest.

"What do you want, greenbacks?"

She thought quickly, twenty-five percent.

Twenty-five—shit, if she helped get his dope to Dresden, she could have forty, wholesale. She did the math—that was like fifteen grand, right? Right, Mitchell said, approximately. Suspicious now, she said, That's the first time anyone bargained up. He brought his hands into a praying position, saying then she'd never been to a fire sale.

Second floor, northeast corner of 431 Howard, Fowler was on all fours, spreading buckskin car coats out on the carpet. Now that he'd found the seams, he knew where to look for the tiny little zippers.

A few feet away, Enid spoke into the phone on her desk. "Yes, Mr. Gall, Ivan will receive a plaque. Thanks again." Hanging up, waiting until Fowler bit.

"You want I should pick a letter?"

Her nostrils contracted—oh, she was going to fix that smartass pose. "Listen, if this adds the way I calculate, we've got the middleman, the supplier, and the grower—the top Sandinista—and I simply love that cowboy from the Hoedown for all three."

"I think he's of Polish descent, Hosowich."

Enid blew that off. "First off, I'm pretty sure he's the one who wrecked my sign. Second, I get a message from Veronica Cake."

"Yet another reliable source. Gotta say, you got the contacts—but hey, ever thought of asking Sweet Daddy Sika who's got the dope?"

"Pimp?"

"Wrestler."

Enid waved dismissively. "Veronica says the cowboy left with the dago ballerina."

Fowler sat back against the soft blue wall. "So far, due respect, you have a cowboy banging a peeler blows the odd roach. I found only two eighths in her coat, possession. And I did run his plates, nothing."

"Thing is, Gall's Hardware has his plates on the list of people buying excessive amounts of African Violet Mix."

"He's a farmer," Fowler said, "grows things."

Enid rummaged in her desk, handing him a faxed magazine article, *High Times*: Fly Higher on African Violet Mix.

"Gall's been doing as all the hardwares were told—taking plates of people buying too much," Enid said. "Hosowich buys five bags, twenty a month later. Tyler's kid, Ivan, wrote it all down, documented."

Fowler rubbed his eyes. He still didn't see how a farmer buying plant food was probable cause, but then what the shit did he know? "Hey," he said. "Can I do it next time?"

Mitchell walked into the living room in baggy Lee painters, towelling his hair. Calling out for the girl, he started procrastinating when she didn't answer. Then he looked out the window, and goddammit if she wasn't riding that horse of his and whipping around a half-assed lasso.

Kicking into Birkenstocks, he shuffled out, mouth open. Catori steered to the pasture's edge, throwing the lasso over his shoulders.

"Where'd you learn that kind of lassoin'?" he said, fighting out of it. "Legace said you done did it to a lawman."

"I'm Ojibway. We work a lot with rope." She smirked, looked down at him, clean without his moustache and grizzle. Rode hard, leathery around the eyes, mouth, but handsome, even if he'd missed the freakin' sign on the road. His hair was bristly now, smelled nice too. Irish Spring, she thought, reaching behind his neck, pulling the collar on his blue-black shirt back to read the label. "What Goes Around—not bad."

"Also by the pound," he said. Pointing at Hasty, "How?"

Catori pressed her lips together.

"Political correct," Mitchell said. "I mean, *how* did you mount her?"

"Like you told me, I just talked to her like a fellow creature, talked her through it and she responded."

Mitchell covered his smile as he spoke. "Well maybe it'd be different if'n there was meat on your breath. And you're so in touch with the animals—how come you ain't never heard of a cow with three horns?"

"I've heard, old-timer, and where I come from it's always birth defects. Now how come your horse won't let you step up?"

Used to be, Mitchell said, Hasty Kiss was a harness racer. A good bet until she stopped up short with a condylar fracture—quack for busting her head.

Over yonder at Windsor Raceway they said she needed eight month's stall rest. Mitchell adopted her for the price of a border hassle, bringing her around in half the time. It's just that, at the track, she was called Bucking Doe, hallmarking her displeasure for people.

"Thinking it was negatory connotations making her mad, I changed her name. She's since simmered some, stopped kicking, but I wouldn't step up." Petting Hasty's snout, "You're a good pet anyway, a friend." She took another nip, Mitchell pulling back. "Maybe I ought to rename you again—Nasty Bitch."

"Talk about negatory."

"You don't know the half of it. Now listen, I got the van all packed before I showered the smell off—everything in airtights, like paint." Looking at her sitting up there, he shielded his eyes from the falling sun. "I am sorry."

She sighed, thinking he must be Catholic or something. "You don't have to be."

"Says who?"

"Mourning Dove. He said every disease has a herb to cure it, every person a mission to grow it—his theory of existence."

"Yeah, and how long did old Mourning *exist*?"

She thought about it. "Forty-eight years."

Mitchell ran a hand over his smooth face, wondering how much time that shave took off him.

Catori sat at the kitchen table, griped about the tofu cabbage rolls, Mitchell shushing her as CKLW returned to Joe Louis Arena. John Scott Dickson had both goals, Windsor up two–zip.

Red Wings' toque in place, Mitchell said they'd listen to the third period enroute to the border—turning on the TV without volume to create moving shadows, guiding Catori outside, down the poorly lit path.

She pulled her wet hair back into a sandstone half cap, saying, "So I'm your Canadian girlfriend and you're a Detroit contractor. You're driving me home after the game—that's our story, simple."

"Should work." He looked at the gap where her vanilla velour hoody didn't quite meet matching velour pants. "Buckets are all marked like paints, sealed like new, stacked nice, plus I got rollers, brushes, masking tape."

"But if they open anything?"

"To the big pasture we're a goin'."

"Better a Canadian prison."

"More like Jackson State." That was a third voice, Enid Bruckner stepping from behind the outhouse, Fowler in tow.

Mitchell sagged. He didn't want to accept he had that there Federale on his ranch, but here she was, smiling her tight smile, pointing her pistol at Catori, mimicking Mitchell. "Looks like she got stirred with a stick, dragged backward, then chewed her split ends off—she worth it?" When Mitchell didn't answer, Enid said, "I want to give the barns a thrice-over, so please, lead me inside."

Mitchell looked over her shoulder, seeing Wolfie chasing Lou over a bale in the moonlight—thanks girls. "Just you mind your pepper box." Laying his eyes on her Les Baer Prowler III. "My horse's crazier than Orville Redenbacher in a micro."

Sure cowboy, Enid said, fine. Following Mitchell and Catori into the bigger barn, Hasty kicking up a fuss in her stall, Enid told Fowler, "Go ahead."

He opened his hands. "What?"

"At the office, you asked could you do it this time?"

"I was kidding."

"Whoa." Mitchell pointed outside. "Dope's in the van, paint cans—you heard me."

Enid looked at Fowler. "Just subdue the suspect."

Oh that's all, only Fowler thought the suspect was cooperating. Enid rolled her eyes, made a noise with her tongue, bringing the gun high above her head, down hard. Mitchell crumpled, Enid booting him in the ribs a few times. Cuffing hands behind his back, she grabbed a roll of duct tape off the workbench, bit a strip off, taping his mouth shut.

Rising from her knees, checking out that horse again, Enid looked around the barn, wondering whether she'd really found the grail after all, or even *a* grail. Dammit, if everything he had was in that van, this wasn't more than a local news brief, a blip—and now what the hell was she hearing outside? Chickens?

Catori slipped into the smaller barn thinking chickens—how could she use the chickens? She couldn't, but there had to be something—anything—and now that misfit cow was agitated, snorting, tusk pumping like a piston. Yeah, that was natural.

Spying a garden hose of rope hanging in the animal's stall, she went in, gingerly stepping around the beast. A bit worried when the cow bolted, but what the hell? Catori's only hope was to cause as much chaos as possible, so yeah, now that she thought of it, she could use the chickens.

"You were covering me, huh?" Enid nodded, pointing her gun at where Catori had been standing. "Thanks, Fowler. Just you run around the barn, back in. She's still out there—find her."

He sighed, clicking the safety on his Glock; seventeen rounds, seventeen more in his peacoat. Careful, ready, he decided to clean this up, blow the whistle when it was over.

Eyes adjusting on the way out, he couldn't see anything at first. But what the shit was it with all those chickens? Chickens, plus he heard something else—footsteps, rapid footsteps from different directions. Christ, what were they? And how many?

Lou knocked him down from behind, Wolfie, the bigger dog, liberating his gun as it fired wildly. One of them yelped. Hit, Fowler thought, picking himself up as the other ran off. Then there were more footsteps, heavier.

Fumbling with plastic Eskimo buttons, Fowler came up with his Bic. Flicking it, hearing something snorting, seeing something coming at him as soon as the flame caught. Talk about birth defects—now what the shit was that?

Inside the barn, Enid called Fowler's name, throwing stuff she couldn't use off the workbench. Finding a flashlight, she stepped outside, casting it.

First she saw the dog side-winding, whimpering, then Fowler being gored up against the barn, shouting, Are you happy now? Shoot it, inbred. Screaming something terrible from deep, down inside by the time she fired.

Simmi was still going good, but Fowler had stopped hollering. Enid had hit *him*, his neck limp.

Simmi staggered, tipping into a heap when Enid stepped closer for a second try. Then Enid went down too, grunting, gripping the lasso around her neck, tight.

Catori scooped the Les Baer, dragging Enid back in the barn, tying the other end of the rope to Hasty Kiss. The animal was kicking mad when Catori dropped the slack. Opening the gate, she fired into the ceiling, sending Hasty clippety-clop into the beautiful Detroit night—more than half a moon, stars everywhere.

Enid tried to say something, but she was frozen, seized up, watching the coil unravel as the girl spoke.

"God took southerly wind, blew his breath, and created horse."

"You're not a dago?" Enid said. Slack gone, rope taunt, she pawed her throat all over again, standing, running until she hit uneven ground a few strides from the door.

Mitchell mumbled something fierce, eyes bulging, as Catori peeled back the tape. Gasping, he pointed outside with his head. "Two dead Federales, my land—we've got to burn the breeze, now."

"What's that mean?" She leaned over, kissing his forehead. "We're in cahoots?"

"Means we got to go, and yeah."

"Yeah what?"

"Cahoots," he said, watching her.

"Right." She looked away. "Cahoots. Only I think that cop still has the keys to your cuffs. And like you said, it's time to burn the breeze...."

Oh man, he could see where this was going.

Time was, this life of Mitchell's was his juice, being the lone hand on his own land. And for a good long while there, he really was his own man.

He'd had quite a run, a good one. But on his knees now, defenseless, hands behind his back, he found himself accusing her of getting greedy, wanting too much. Like that Paul Newman in *Hud*—he wanted daddy's farm so bad every critter was destroyed by the time he got to be big sugar. Then he said she simply couldn't pull it off alone. And Legace, he wasn't going to be okay with this. Same time, Mitchell thought, all that really did make him sound like a mail-order cowboy, nor was it helping.

Ah, maybe he could have lived another life or at least've gotten out while the getting was good—put the land to use, legally. Maybe even researched that old stone and turned the place into a fine, upstanding tourist trap. Maybe, but then he just looked at Catori and shrugged, saying, "What came first, young lady, grants or farmers?"

Great Minds
by Barbara Fradkin

During her career as a child psychologist, Barbara Fradkin saw much of the bleaker side of life. Many of her clients probably had their own dark visions of revenge. That knowledge colours much of Barbara's writing, particularly her short fiction, as demonstrated in the previous Insomniac Press anthologies *Iced* and *Hard Boiled Love*. Now a full-time writer, Barbara continues to produce highly respected work. She was a double nominee for the 2001 Arthur Ellis Award for Best Short Story and has received praise for her novels about Ottawa Police Inspector Michael Green. The fourth Inspector Green book, *Fifth Son*, will be released this fall by Rendezvous Press.

I was in no hurry to kill him. My back ached and the cold earth chilled my bones, but a good murder takes time in the plotting. So I spied on him in the mornings as he bounded out of the house, whistled down the walk and climbed into his hunter-green Mercedes. I spied on the girl too, the final nail in his coffin, the living proof of who he was. I watched her totter down the steps on her platform shoes, juggling books, flute case and band jacket as she scrambled in beside him. Some days he threatened to leave without her and I could hear them bicker all the way down the drive and past the cedars where I crouched.

The third morning he left the car behind and walked by me on his way down the street, passing so close I could see the arrogant arch of his brow and the ice blue of his eyes. I hunched lower. How easy it would have been to deliver one quick knife thrust through his heart. Easier still to aim a tiny .22-calibre pistol through the branches right between those wintry eyes. But I needed a safer escape route. Among the commuters heading off to work and children trailing along the sidewalk, someone was sure to notice a strange young woman fleeing on foot down the residential street in broad daylight. This murder had to be perfect. I had even taken care to get off the bus blocks from the house and slip up the street at five-thirty in the morning, before even the earliest fanatics were out with their dogs. Nothing connected me to this man, so if I escaped the murder scene undetected, no one would think to suspect me. Except possibly my grandmother, but her few brain cells were so pickled by alcohol I doubt she even realized what she'd said. Besides, she'd merely given me a list of names in response to my casual probing, and it was my detective work that had put the pieces together.

My grandmother, the silly bitch, had thought she was doing me a favour when she tracked me down through the Children's Aid Society to tell me about my mother. But I had already figured out all I wanted to about my real parents and I carried them nestled safe and comforting in my soul. They explained so much to me. They made me feel as if somewhere, on some plane in another life, I belonged.

From the earliest I can remember, I had always felt like an outsider in the Russell family. In a house full of brunettes, I was blond. Tall and wispy when everyone else was fat, aloof and contemplative when everyone else raced in circles. I remember doing multiplication tables in my head while my older brother was struggling to count to five, reading *Goosebumps* and Stephen King before he had even mastered Dr. Seuss. My mother—for that's who I thought she was—even bought me books, a new concept for her, and my father delighted in my recall of hockey statistics. I was their little freak, and even they admitted they could never have created me.

They gave me some bizarre labels like Our Gift from God and Miracle Child, but it wasn't until my mother returned from her first interview with my grade-three teacher that she admitted the truth. She was smiling so broadly I thought her bovine face would split.

"I've never heard such praise from a teacher in all my years!" she exclaimed, crushing me into her thick, smelly arms. She could never understand how my bird-like spirit preferred to fly free and out of reach. I'd read about adoption in one of my books and it seemed to explain so much that I asked her directly if I was adopted. She took a long time to answer, foolish enough to think I'd be devastated. She didn't realize what a relief it was to have an explanation for my sense of alienation. I belonged somewhere else.

I badgered her endlessly to know who my parents were, why they had given me up, and whether I had any siblings. I pictured myself with a sister, younger and not as smart, but slavish in her devotion.

"I don't know anything, Sarah," the woman who called herself my mother said at first. But I didn't believe her. In her clumsy haste to reassure me, she had let slip that my parents had not abandoned me, so she had to know something. I played up that theme in the weeks that followed.

"Of course they abandoned me," I said one afternoon with my most waif-like pout. "Why else would I be here with you?"

"But I love you, honey! I've loved you since the first moment they brought you to me to foster. And I fought like hell when they wanted to take you away—"

I forced myself to snuggle in her arms. They should be another woman's arms, a delicate blond woman with dancing eyes and a wit as sharp as mine. I leaned my head on Mrs. Russell's shoulder. "But they didn't fight back, that's what I mean. That's why children get adopted. Because their real parents don't want them. Or else—" I stopped before my next thought popped out of my mouth, but my look of dismay must have shown, because she wrapped those smelly arms more tightly.

"Oh honey, it wasn't like that. Your mother would have come for you if she could. But she...she was killed."

She denied knowing further details, but a little more pathetic whimpering wore her down. She stroked my hair with a heavy hand. "I don't know how she died, honey. But she must have been very smart, like you. And I'm sure she was very brave. However she was killed, I bet she died trying to do something very important."

By eight years of age I had already erected some fairly high barriers against hope, but in spite of myself, a small kernel of joy began to swell inside me. I folded Mrs. Russell's words into my fantasies, nurtured them and gave them life. My mother had been brave and smart, she must have been. She had been engaged in some important cause which had cost her her life. She had not abandoned me, she had loved me to her grave. My heart sang.

Over the years I slowly added detail and texture to my dream, sculpting a vision of my family that included a father, an enduring love affair, and a noble sacrifice in the service of mankind. Perhaps my mother had been a nurse—no, surely a doctor—caring for the sick and wretched in some dangerous hellhole in the world. Central America...no, Africa. She had met my father, a fellow doctor, and amid the pain and despair they had fallen in love. When civil war broke out, they rushed to fly me out to safety, but there was no room on the plane for them.

The more vivid my dream family became, the less I needed the Russells. Mrs. Russell kept up her primitive overtures to make me feel part of the crude, raucous household in which I lived, but I had another home, deep inside myself. When the Russells sat around the TV watching *Roseanne* reruns and cackling with hilarity at the infantile antics, or when my father and brother cheered some steroid Neanderthal on Saturday-morning wrestling, I would travel to Africa. There, my real mother and I would sit on the veranda of our modest cottage, sipping mango juice and listening to the screech of monkeys and macaws, and my mother would tell me about her search for exotic plant cures. My real father would join us and we would discuss our upcoming trip to Cairo to see the pyramids and the tombs of the Pharaohs. We would laugh at the foibles of the Greek gods and ponder the wisdom of Maimonides. My parents would know the answers to all my questions and there would be no noisy, bumbling brother to burst into the middle of our talks, full of flatulence and drool with not a neuron to be seen.

I pored over encyclopaedias and old newspapers, ferreting out information on Africa to learn all I could about the life they might have led. I learned about the work of Doctors Without Borders and even wrote to a few doctors in the hopes of giving my dream parents substance. I don't know at what age my vague yearnings crystallized into certainty, but by the time I was eleven I was determined to become a doctor. I felt as if I had been given a great legacy. I would pick up the fight where my parents had fallen, so the tyrants of the world would not win. That hope became my guiding light. I spent my teenage years reading up on science and medicine the way an athlete stokes up on steroids to have a head start out of the gate.

I had flown through high school in three years and was in my second year of pre-med when my grandmother's letter arrived. Actually the letter was from the CAS, informing me that my maternal grandmother had made a request to establish contact with me. I left it unanswered for days because I couldn't think straight. By then I had isolated myself in a mini-fortress of self-sufficiency in my upstairs bedroom, cocooned in books, computer and dreams, and I was unsure I wanted to let anyone in. Especially someone whose truth and reality might dethrone the dream family I carried inside.

Need finally won out over fear. Perhaps my grandmother's truth would be even better than my dream. Perhaps she would even have a picture of my parents that I could prop on the corner of the desk where I sat every night. I phoned the social worker to set up a meeting with my grandmother on the neutral grounds of a doughnut shop the next afternoon. I arrived ten minutes late, wanting to be sure she was there and giving myself the opportunity to size her up before making contact. If I didn't like my first impression, I would simply walk back out the door, my dreams still intact.

How I wish I had done that. But I didn't. When I pushed open the glass door of the doughnut shop, I saw no one who matched my image of my grandmother. No kindly and energetic old lady with omniscient eyes. Only truck drivers, harried mothers, whining children and in the corner, bent over her cigarette, an obese woman with doughy skin, bleached hair and a threadbare coat. She squinted at me through curls of smoke and a faint apprehension lit her pouchy eyes. Drawn as if by a magnet of disbelief, I approached.

"Sarah?" she asked in a voice shredded by decades of smoke.

I sat down in the chair opposite, my heart pounding. Tears filled her rheumy eyes and her flesh quivered. "I've waited so long. I got so many questions." Her eyes raked over me, pig-like amid folds of flesh. "You don't look a thing like her."

"There must be some mistake. The wrong Sarah, the wrong baby—"

She shook her head. "The CAS checked it all out. Checked me out real good too before they let me see you."

"But the CAS couldn't find you years ago. They said there were no surviving relatives."

The woman who called herself my grandmother stared at me through hardening eyes. "Is that what they told you? The bitches. They always thought they knew what was good for you—never mind your own flesh and blood!" Her hand shot out to clutch my arm. "What else did the bitches tell you?"

I resisted the urge to bolt from the table. Laying bare my cherished family to this tawdry crone felt like a sacrilege. "Not much. My foster mother told me my mother was killed."

Quick tears blurred the daggers in her eyes. She sat back and scavenged in her grimy purse for another cigarette. Only once she lit it did she nod. "We didn't just dump you, y'know. Your mother loved you. Always. And me too. That's the truth. After she died, I—well, I wasn't good for much, I admit. But that tight-assed social worker..." She inhaled smoke deep into her lungs as if it were the very breath of life. For a moment she waged her own private war with rage and pain, then she sighed. "Your mother was a good person. I want you to know that. She was trying to get her life straight, raise you right. The way she died, naked, tied up like that in that alley—the Children's Aid tried to make out like she was a bad mother."

I no longer heard the words. Her slack lips undulated, exposing jagged yellow teeth, but I heard nothing above the bewilderment in my head. The lips undulated, the confusion swirled. "Stop it!" I finally heard myself say. "What are you talking about?"

"Your mother's murder. She wasn't a whore like the papers made out. She didn't have a string of men. She worked in that bar to put food on the table and guys were always hitting on her. Some asshole didn't like it when she said no."

After years of living in my alien world, I had perfected the art of mind over emotion and had become adept at channelling pain and confusion into locked storage vaults in my mind. Reason was my most potent asset, and I summoned it now to push my thoughts back into place. "She was murdered here in the city? When?"

"Fifteen years ago. And the bastard that did it was never caught. The cops never had a fucking clue."

"Do you?"

She shook her thick jowls. "She was a good kid. She didn't have it easy and I'm not saying she didn't make mistakes, but she shoulda got her second chance."

"What do you mean?"

"She was going back to school. Wanted to get her high school and then maybe learn computers or that. School wasn't her favourite thing, you know, but she was going to give it another try, 'cause of you. She saw how smart you were, even as a little kid. I hope you stuck it out and got your high school."

The lunacy of the idea almost made me laugh aloud despite the outrage beating at the doors of my mind. I was in university on a full scholarship, with my eye set on the best medical school that could offer the same. None of this made any sense. "What about my father? Could he have killed her?"

My grandmother sucked the last wisp of smoke from her cigarette butt and crushed it with pudgy fingers. "He wasn't in the picture. Karen—she never said who he was."

Meaning she didn't know, I thought, as a fresh wave of outrage battered my mind. I felt my resistance slipping, the storage vaults bulging. The smoke, the stale beer, the stained and tattered coat and the stink of unwashed body turned my stomach. Oblivious to this, my grandmother raised her bloodshot eyes sadly. "Just so you know, we loved you. They taking good care of you? You look skinny."

I managed to babble some inanity and shoved my chair back with a hasty glance at my watch. Promising to be in touch, I gathered the shreds of my dream about me and fled.

For two days I studied harder and longer than I had ever studied before. I could have confronted my adoptive mother or phoned the CAS to demand confirmation, but that would have betrayed how important my dream family was to me. After two days I settled down to research my real mother for myself. The newspapers from fifteen years ago were full of the gruesome account, complete with photos of trash cans and boarded windows in the alley where she was found. Karen Moffat had been one of life's losers from the start, shunted from cheap homes to boarding houses to shelters and back during her childhood, on the streets at sixteen and dead at twenty. Her five brothers and sisters spoke to reporters eagerly, some from their crumbling front stoops and others from their jail cells. Karen was an innocent, they insisted, just looking for someone to love her and hold her. Her baby was the first human love she had ever really had and she would never have done anything to put the baby in danger. She wanted to find a day job and a decent man, to build a home and give her daughter a normal life.

Because she was supposed to be my mother, I tried to relate to this pathetic waif. I certainly had encountered enough like her in the public housing project where I lived, people full of yearnings, hopes and flashes of goodness who ricocheted from one relationship and experience to another without the brains or mind control to right their course. But I lived in another dimension. Although I could find no footing now in my fantasy of doctors, bravery and martyrdom, neither could I ground myself amid the deadbeats and petty criminals I was reading about.

One newspaper carried a sad, grainy photo of my mother, sheets of lank black hair framing a shy face with a tentative smile and buck teeth. Not me at all. From what I could surmise, not a single gene from this pathetic woman had found expression in me. As if I had materialized from thin air.

Which, of course, was absurd. One of my real mother's sisters had been very forthcoming on the subject of my paternity and her musings were extensively quoted in the local tabloid. "Karen liked to party. She used to keep company with five, maybe ten guys in a month, and she didn't keep close track of things. But having a baby changed all that. Having a girl, you know?"

But this same sister swore my mother wasn't a prostitute. Her bedmates were simply party animals like herself, culled from the drinkers and deadbeats she met in the bar. Not a college degree among them. Instinctively I knew none of these could be my father. Conquering my revulsion, I contacted my grandmother again. Where might my mother have met an educated man, I asked? Maybe a doctor, a businessman, even a university student? One might have come into the bar, she replied, but only if he was slumming, because the bar was in Mechanicsville.

I thought of Mechanicsville, a neighbourhood where generations of working toughs shared the narrow streets with drug dealers, prostitutes and the occasional crack house. "Were any of the guys she hung out with really smart?"

I could hear her wheezing through the phone lines as the brain cells clicked slowly over. Finally she rasped, "Well, there was a kid—Sammy Gilmore—he finished high school, he was working in a bank. And Jesse Somebody, I think he finished high school too. Oh wait, the police were nosing around Stephano Luciano. His dad owned a fancy Italian restaurant and Stephano was in college, I remember that."

Stephano Luciano wasn't difficult to track down, but I spent several evenings nibbling antipasto in the corner of his fancy Preston Street restaurant—one of several now—before he appeared. Dancing dark eyes, untameable black curls and a short, stocky frame that was just beginning to balloon. Surely not my father.

Discouraged, I was paying my bill and preparing to leave when the restaurant door opened and in walked a trio of men, elegant in designer golf shirts and leather moccasins. Stephano hopped around the bar with a cry of delight, hugged them all heartily and joined them at a table in the corner. I sank slowly back into my chair. It was a very slim hope, but if Stephano had been in college nineteen years ago, perhaps he had partied with some of his friends and introduced them to my mother. Friends he kept in touch with even to this day.

I counted my remaining money and ordered the cheapest entree on the menu. For the next hour I studied the three men, listening to their banter and analyzing their moves. From the beginning, my attention was caught by the tallest of the three, a long-limbed blond with fluid hands, a patrician brow and cobalt blue eyes. They called him Richard. He held himself aloof, smiling occasionally but rarely joining in the boisterous laughter of the others. When he spoke, his voice was so quiet I couldn't hear him, but the others stopped as if to cling to his every word.

At one point, his eyes caught mine over the rim of his cappuccino and a faint frown drew his brows together. Aware that I might be dealing with an intelligence even greater than mine and fearing discovery, I paid and slipped out to wait in the shadows by the front door. Barely a minute passed before he emerged and paused to scan the sidewalk as if searching for something. I pressed further into the shadows until he shrugged and set off down the street, keys jingling. I followed warily and watched him climb into a shiny new Mercedes.

I have few friends at the university—few friends anywhere, for I haven't the time—but I have plenty of like-minded acquaintances who love a good challenge. I handed the licence-plate number over to one of them and by the next day I had a name and address from his computer. Richard Mathers, of an exclusive Rockcliffe address. A search of the Internet connected the man to dozens of erudite articles and associations in the area of forensic psychiatry. Now I recognized the name from frequent newspaper articles. Richard Mathers held dual degrees in law and medicine and was head of forensic psychiatry at the university medical school as well as the local psychiatric hospital. He provided expert testimony in the trials of countless murderers and sex offenders across the country. A very intelligent and powerful man.

I sat at the computer terminal, excitement bubbling in my throat. Perhaps I was the daughter of a doctor after all, a crusader in his own way against the evil in our midst. Hiding the tremor in my hands, I printed out a few of his articles to read in the privacy of my room. They revealed a man with a profound intellect and an abiding fascination with the darker corners of man's soul.

"The psychopath," he wrote, "sees himself as the centre of the universe, and others as mere obstacles or assets to the attainment of his will. Typically he kills for personal gain, when another human being stands between him and something he wants. To this extent, his behaviour may be seen as different from the normal in degree rather than in kind. Normal men too will kill for personal gain, if the danger or the reward is great enough. However, the crucial difference lies in the subsequent experience of remorse. A normal man may be haunted by guilt and flashbacks for years after the act, whereas the psychopath will barely give it a second thought."

Over the next few days I pored over books and journals in the medical library to learn all I could about the man who might be my father. Objectively I knew this was irrational. I had followed the most tenuous threads of logic and coincidence to pin my hopes on a tall, lean, blond man with a natural reserve and a genius IQ.

Born the only son and great hope of a divorced hairdresser, he had financed his way through undergraduate school with scholarships and tips from waiting tables at local restaurants. In 1977 he had won a generous scholarship to Johns Hopkins Medical School, followed in 1981 by a psychiatric residency at the internationally renowned and highly sought-after Maudsley Hospital in London. With that pedigree after his name, his future was assured.

Nineteen seventy-seven was the year I was conceived, and 1981 the year my mother was murdered. I stared in dawning horror at the coincidences arrayed before me. A psychopath kills for personal gain, but a normal man does too, if the danger or reward are great enough. What greater reward than a residency in the most prestigious psychiatric hospital in the world? And what greater danger than a barmaid with a three-year-old accident to support?

Deep inside, I began to formulate my plan. It was my secret family story, it would be my secret resolution. The police, faced with an allegation against one of the most brilliant and respected men in the country, would laugh my string of coincidences and suppositions right out of the station. If this man were truly my father, and if he had chosen his ambitions over the future of his daughter and the very life of her mother, I intended to have the last laugh.

That lingering question was answered on my first visit to his house the next afternoon. A girl of about thirteen sat painting her toenails on the front stoop of the massive stone mansion. Well disguised by my bicycle helmet and sunglasses, I feigned confusion, stopped my bike and called to her for directions. When she looked up, I saw myself. Younger, half formed like a yearling doe, but unmistakably me. I pedalled away with no feeling in my limbs. There she sat on that flagstone step, surrounded by lush lawns and flowers, with three cars in the driveway and walls of books visible through the glass. That should be me. But instead, when my mother, naive wretch that she was, approached him with the news of the beautiful bright little girl they had created, she had signed her own death warrant.

Physician, heal thyself. Or at least know thyself. Was that the reason for his choice of specialty? Did the murder of my mother haunt him? I wondered as I watched him those next few mornings. Not enough to slow him down, clearly, but in the darkness just before sleep, did he think of me? Did he ever wonder what had become of me? Did he carry me nestled somewhere in his heart, as I had always carried him?

The fourth morning of my vigil, he was late and as I peered through the cedars impatient for the sight of him, a new idea began to germinate. He had probably always pictured me as a replica of my mother, not of him. Perhaps he would be happy to meet me, proud to know how intelligent and successful I was. What a credit I was to his name.

How simple it would be to cross the street, mount the walk and ring the doorbell. Yet fear held me back. Not of him, of course, but of losing this last vestige of my dream. What if he had forgotten my very existence and was angry at being reminded? I scanned back through my memory of the essays he had written on human nature, searching for scraps of guilt and longing, all the while berating myself for my weakness in spirit. I didn't need a father, I told myself. I had managed for years with nothing but a fantasy for comfort and inspiration. I didn't—

"Hello, Sarah."

I spun around, branches scraping my back. Behind me, a dapper figure had parted the cedars and I found myself looking up into an older mirror of myself. He squatted on the dank earth, matter-of-fact. No explanations were needed, no lies offered. He had discovered me. Perhaps it was that brief glimpse in the restaurant, but more likely he had known about me all along.

"Well, Sarah," he said quietly, in a voice rich with confidence. "You can do one of two things. You can turn me in, or you can let me help you get into the finest medical school on the continent. Pity to waste those brains."

I searched his ice-blue eyes for feeling or fear, but found nothing. He looked through me, didn't see me. In that instant I realized that he had not given my mother a second thought, nor me either. I was an obstacle to him, nothing more. And he had figured out exactly as I had that nothing connected me to him and no one would suspect him in my death.

I held his dead eyes, hoping he wouldn't see the hardening in mine. I could be patient. Someday, somehow, I would find the perfect way to exact revenge. But for now, I put on my sweetest Faustian smile. I was his daughter, after all.

"How about Harvard?"

The Big Trip
by John Swan

A native of Hamilton, Ontario, John Swan is the reigning godfather of Canuck Noir. Co-editor of the anthologies *Iced* and *Hard Boiled Love*, John also writes tough, raw fiction that explores the darkness of the Canadian soul. His short fiction has appeared in numerous periodicals and anthologies. A collection of linked stories *The Rouge Murders* was published in 1996. His new novel *Sap* was published by Insomniac Press in 2003. Writing in the *Globe and Mail*, Margaret Cannon says Swan delivers "the essentials of noir in a distinctively Canadian style...he has the manner down."

"Take your hand out of my pocket, sonny."

"Ain't no hand in your pocket. Bumpy road is all."

The kid moved quick. Enough that Nelson, waking, couldn't be sure.

"Just because you saw the driver stow my walker doesn't make me an easy mark. I know your tricks."

"Yeah? What tricks you know?"

Nelson rolled his eyes. "Chicago Bump. Detroit Deke." They might have been dance steps for all Nelson knew. He pulled glasses up from the string on his chest, hooked them over his nose at a serious angle, slid back to his side of the two-wide seat. The kid looked maybe sixteen, maybe eighteen. Or twenty. The glasses were an old prescription. The kid was no more than twenty-five, young enough to be impressed, Nelson hoped. "Don't even think trying the St. Louis Slide around me."

"The Windsor Withhold."

"Windsor Withhold?"

"More a grift than a grab," the kid said. "Guy up north perfected it to scam cash machines. Since your time probably. You were on the grift?"

Nelson took a second look over the top of his glasses. "Philly Flip, Miami Move, the Seattle Shake. Sure, I've been there and back."

The kid grinned, pearly white. "Toledo Two-Step."

Nelson revealed his own incisors, the best government would buy. "Don't believe I know that one." But he did. You do the Toledo Two-Step when you close the bars on a cold, February night, forgetting to take a final whiz and find you've locked your keys in the car, or you can't find a cab, or the buses have stopped running this side of town. Every city had its variant: the Chi-Town Cha Cha; the Montreal Mambo, the Buffalo Boogaloo.

"Tell me how it runs," thinking he had the kid now.

"Two guys in a line, like getting off the bus. One old, one young, mark in between. Old guy keels, grabs the mark on his way down and hangs on wheezing while the young guy lifts the mark's wallet and any luggage that's loose."

"Youngster rabbits. Mark dogs him while the old guy grifts the cops."

The kid dipped his near shoulder. "If you're country. In the Bigs the old guy takes the pass and holds sliding away."

"Huh," Nelson said. "Needs polish."

"Why I'm talking to you, old-timer." The kid held out a paw. The bus lurched left, changing lanes. "Delisle. Delisle Hoskins."

He was more shirt than man, blue with a darker blue check, and a yellow bandana over his skull, knotted at the back. A gold chain hung from the extended wrist, but the smile looked bright and sincere.

"Nelson Mandela." Nelson pumped the kid's hand once. Kid didn't bat an eye. He was good or he was dumb. But right now he was a bother. "Shouldn't you be on a street corner somewhere selling crack?"

"No future in it," Delisle said. "Looking for something with a bit of romance, and the possibility of travel."

Nelson leaned close enough the kid might name his brand of mouthwash. "Tell me Delisle: are there no other seats on this bus?"

"Sure," stretching his neck out into the dark divide between the sleeping passengers. "Sixty maybe. But they all got somebody in 'em."

"And could one of them be a quiet, skinny little Sunday-school teacher you might trade places with?"

"Might maybe. Twenty bucks, I could try waking her up."

"Now that," Nelson sighed, "that would be the Baton Rouge Rollover."

"You say so."

Nelson looked at his watch. "How far you going, Delisle?"

"Far as I need to get ahead. You?"

"Cleveland."

"You kidding me? This bus goes through to Chicago. Nothing in Cleveland that ain't bigger and better in Chi. I be seeing my eggs over easy in the Ohio Open Kitchen tomorrow morning."

"My brother lives in Cleveland. I need to see him before I die," thinking that sitting next to death might shift the kid to another piece of Greydog upholstery, all else having failed. "First time in fifty-plus years."

"How come? You guys have a fight or something? Years since you spoke? Can't rest till you make it up? Like that?"

"Do I look like I'm side-saddle on a riding mower?"

"That movie, right? *Getting Straight*, something like that. Yeah, I seen that on cable. Bit slow, you ask me."

"It was a story, Delisle, not mine, but a story. That's all."

"I dig it. Give the mark something to believe in. Why I like you old guys is your stories, instead all the time smash and grab. Your time had finesse." He stretched out the "sss" as he stretched down into the seat. "So Nelson, what *is* your story?"

The bus swayed back to its own lane. Nelson swayed with it. He'd been under for an hour forty-five. Pretty much as long as he could sleep at one stretch these days anyway. "You're not going to let it rest, are you."

"It's a long trip, you don't talk to nobody."

"We were the same age, exactly."

"Like twins?"

"Identical. And once we figured out the teachers couldn't tell us apart, we had the world by its tender bits. Teachers passed us through just to get rid of us and we graduated to John Law. Coppers knew there was the two of us, but they could never pin anything on one when the other might have done it. Nobody could say for sure. Didn't hurt that the old man was city alderman either. We had things so smooth we didn't even notice we'd outgrown home. The coppers noticed though. Soon as the old man lost an election a squad of beat-bullies stamped us onto a postcard and mailed us out of town, no return address."

"Cops."

"Same everywhere, but I'm not crying. Justice is a franchise, just like McDonald's. It's more important to be familiar than to be good. Figure what bets are already covered and by who, you can make your mark wherever you go. Pretty soon we had action for any town big enough to host a pool hall and a four-pump gas station. I hustled the felt while Horatio — that was my brother—knocked over the station, prodding the gas jockey with a pool cue in case the local law was too dumb to look for the usual suspects in the usual places. We quick had it timed so the RCMP arrived just as my stick hicks figured they'd been hustled and grew restless. I'd have them so mad they'd fight each other to alibi me while the Horsemen tried to put me in a stick-up the other side of town. More than one night we slipped away leaving the locals in a brawl."

"The RCMP? Guys with red coats and horses?"

"That stuff's just for show now. Back then there were still some places men went that machines couldn't. Horses had their role."

"Always get their man."

Nelson laughed. "Yeah, well, not us, not then. There were close calls, I won't say otherwise. Law was slow in Medicine Hat, out gathering prairie muffins maybe when the call came in. That's how I met Suzette Rominski, the little nursie who was stitching the cut under my eye by the time Horatio doubled back for me and figured out where I was. He walked straight into the hospital emergency while she cut the thread. I could see in her eyes she figured right away what was going on and never let on. Not to us. Not to the cops. She was no flat-foot floozie, but she was all over floy floy. You know what that is, floy floy? Means she had "it," with shifafa on the side. I still feel her soft hands on my face.

"I wrote her on and off. We set a weekend up in Calgary. Calgary was where our run ended. Stampede week, the town full of cowboys gassing up and shooting stick, cash like to fall out of their pockets. Horatio and I figured to score big beyond the cattle-yards then hole up in the Palliser Hotel downtown for the Stampede. Suzette already had a room waiting for me. But the cops must have had a conference or something before we got there because they sure saw us coming. Scooped me up from the pool hall with a nod from the manager and Horatio already handcuffed in back of the squad car they threw me in. Saturday and Sunday I'm in keep instead of in the hotel keeping Suzette warm. Monday morning the judge had a whole list of complaints from our travels around his province.

"They still had the same problem of course: which one of us had done what, but without the old man to slow them down they were inclined to be arbitrary. Judge gave us a choice, enlist in the army or wait in jail while the authorities sorted the two of us out. The war was on and I told Horatio I'd sooner be in it than Stoney Mountain."

"The war? You were in Nam?"

Nelson sniffed. "The Big One, before that. Doubleyew, Doubleyew Two. We made London for the Blitz. You heard about the Blitz, eh? And don't say it's a Jewish pancake. Luftwaffe raining bombs down on the city nearly every night, folks sleeping in the subways, scared shitless. Left the streets easy pickings for a couple of lads not frightened by a bit of noise and flash. We were stationed north, but came into The Big Smoke every chance. People locked up when they could, but they couldn't always because buildings left standing had been shaken until nothing was square. Door latches didn't fit the frames, and if they did it only took an army boot and Bob's your uncle, blackout and anyone above ground too busy fighting fire to notice or hear.

"Only let-down was the Brits had nothing to steal, those that stayed in the city anyway. Bit of family silver plate now and again, the odd cherished memento, cigarette money at best. We were starting to figure that, me in the front room of a three-room flat looking over the dusty furniture and thinking, Why bother? when a bomb hit close outside, blowing in what must have been the last intact pane in the city.

"Windows were shuttered during the Blitz. I don't know what happened to the one that caught me, whether the shutters'd been blown off, or they came in with the window. I hadn't even noticed with the heavy, blackout drapes pulled. Might have been the drapes that saved me, a thousand shards of glass shooting across the room. Or maybe luck. Dumb luck. All I know is Horatio had been in back. It was years before I found he'd got out with a smashed hand. When I came around in hospital I had no identification, no idea who or where I was."

The bus slowed, easing off the highway, ramping toward Cleveland city centre.

"I hadn't written Suzette since we'd gone overseas, and now that I needed to I couldn't. What would I tell her? That my face was being rebuilt, along with my memory? Much as they could back then. That I didn't look anything like the buck she'd almost corralled in Calgary? That I wasn't going to be able to support her while I went through years of surgery and rehab? Doesn't seem the way you propose to the woman you love, does it? But it was thinking about that little nursie from The Hat got me through the worst of it."

Delisle sat quietly, the bus mumbling at a red light, plotting its final turns through the dark streets.

"One eye's good, the other glass," Nelson said, leaning to glare into Delisle's startled face. "Can you tell which?"

Delisle turned away.

"Doesn't matter. They both look almost the same now. Let my hair grow, a beard and in the dark you don't notice the face isn't quite what you'd expect. So I can't complain. Not about that.

"They shipped me home year, year-and-a-half later. By home I mean back to Canada, not back to the old man. Then years in hospitals, I didn't want to see anybody from my old life. Didn't want them to see me. I was in Toronto for more surgery when someone, an orderly or a nurse, caught my name: 'Congratulations. You're the father of twin baby boys.' 'Impossible,' I said. 'I only just got here.' 'Twiss,' he says, 'on the maternity-ward records. Father: Nelson.'

"That was me all right. Nelson Twiss isn't such a common name you don't go check to see what's up. I was to be operated on next morning, but I slipped out of my room soon as the dinner trays were cleared, down to maternity. He didn't recognize me. My own brother didn't even turn for a second look after passing me in the hall outside the elevator. I followed him to her private room. He stopped at the open door and looked in. Suzette looked up from their two, suckling babes. 'Hello Nelson,' she said. 'Boys, say hello to your father. Isn't he handsome?' I almost answered when she caught a glimpse of me hanging in behind and gasped. I was gone before Horatio turned 'round."

The bus hissed brake air, releasing Nelson and Delisle from its momentum. Passengers were already standing, removing coats, bags, packages from overhead. Nelson began to shift in his seat.

"He took your name, went home and married Suzette," Delisle said.

"Got it in one."

"What'd you do?"

"Checked myself out of hospital that night. Moved to Montreal. Hired a detective to keep track now and again but never went back to Toronto. Horatio had a good job in a branch plant of some big American company. The kind of job that won't get your hands dirty. Maybe the old man helped him out; I don't know. Probably the old man wanted nothing to do with either of us. I needed to leave it alone, but I never could, quite. Horatio took my papers from the London rubble, see? Had to. And left me there."

Nelson watched passengers disembark, rushing to the terminal, to waiting cabs, to the greeting arms of relatives.

"Every few years I'd phone his company to find out where Horatio—Nelson—was. Pretty soon he'd worked his way into head office here in Cleveland."

Nelson nodded at Delisle to move. He used the seat-backs to support himself down the aisle. The driver waited at the door with his walker pulled from under the bus. Nelson began his measured shuffle into the terminal.

"So now you get together at the end of your lives, all is forgiven?" Delisle tagging along.

"Thought you were going through to Chicago."

The boy shrugged. He'd pulled a yellow/black, insulated jacket, five sizes too big, from the overhead storage rack. The coat was made for shrugging. "I could. I got ten minutes. Or I can hang with you a while. It's an open ticket." He shrugged again. Or maybe it was just the coat. "Finish the story."

"What's with the big clothes? I've rented apartments had less space."

"I make fun of your threads? You're not exactly stylin' these days, case you haven't caught yourself in a mirror lately."

Nelson stopped. "Oh I respect your style, Delisle, believe me. You could hide enough equipment in there to crack a Chubb. Only I thought you fancied yourself a grifter, not a safe buster."

"Finish your story, don't be worrying mine. Plenty of time to write my story."

"My story's pretty much done. You'd be surprised how free that makes a person feel, Delisle."

Delisle swung around front, gripped the walker, blocking Nelson's path, size fifteen spotless white sneakers gripping terrazzo. "Free for what? Come on man, finish."

Nelson sighed. "You tell nobody what you're about to hear. Not for a week, at least."

"Man, how'm I going to promise that when I don't know what it is?"

"Your choice. You want to hear the end or not?"

Delisle let go the walker. Nelson pulled on the hip pocket of his own loose trousers, where he'd first imagined Delisle's hand, showing the grip of an old army revolver. "I swore, if there's only one thing I get out of this life, it's to see Horatio dead before me."

"No, you can't do that man. That's bad karma."

Nelson began a shift around Delisle. "I appreciate the concern, I really do, but it's my story coming to an end, not yours. Anyway, what do you care, living outside the law the way you do?"

"I take people's money, that's it. Never killed nobody." His voiced dropped to a whisper. "And what's money? Pieces of paper. Not even that. Blips on a computer screen. Plenty more where that come from. But murder? Man's only got one life."

"You're a lover I suppose, not a fighter."

"Like that."

"I never got to be a lover, Delisle. I had other women but Suzette was the one I thought about long nights in the hospital wards. Horatio took even that from me, along with the rest of my life. Seems only fair I should get what's left of his."

"What about her? What's this gonna do to Suzette?"

Delisle held the door to the terminal building. Nelson passed through, leaving behind the rumble and hiss of nesting busses, the metallic coo of announced arrivals and departures. Nelson waited before the second rank of doors.

"Horatio's already done it. Suzette's been dead, must be a dozen years. More. An accident or a bug, I don't know. He took her on a business trip, a place where medicine isn't what it is here. She'd be alive if it'd happened here. He should have known better. That was the hardest time. I wanted to kill him then."

"But you didn't, see? You're not a killer, not really."

Nelson stood before the inner door to the terminal. "You going to open that too or do I have to wrestle it myself?"

Delisle hustled round him and pulled the handle on the second door. Nelson started up again.

"But man, you don't want to spend your last days in jail, do you?"

Nelson stopped, looked the boy in the eye. "Now that's what I meant by being free. How much time you think I've left to serve, Delisle?" He started on again.

"Well, what about me? Think how this affects me. I'm young. I'm impressionable. I shouldn't be hearing this." Delisle tried his best smile. "I need a proper education."

"Lesson's over. Everything I got to tell you is stale dated."

"You sure do talk though. You tell some tricks. I could learn from you."

Nelson turned, scanning rows of empty, wooden, bench seats as his head came around. He wanted to sit but needed momentum. Momentum he couldn't get with this kid tugging his sleeve. He pulled his lips back. "That's all it is. Talk. I've told you a story, a good one. Look into my eyes." He shifted his gaze back and forth across Delisle's face. "Still think one of them's glass? Pull my beard. Go ahead, pretend I'm Santa, you're on my knee. Ow! Satisfied? A story. Passed the time didn't it? That's what you wanted, so you said. That's what I gave you. I'm here to visit my grandkids. Now I'm going to go over there," pointing to a bank of payphones, "call them to come pick me up, and I haven't got wind left for you and them both. So screw off and leave me to it. Got it?"

Delisle stood as Nelson slowly moved to the phones. He lifted a handset, took a ruffled notebook from his pocket and flitted pages. He'd started to dial when he noticed Delisle still watching.

"Ssst," he said, nodding toward an approaching security guard. Delisle caught the implied threat, drifted away. Nelson liked the kid well enough, but he'd accuse Delisle of harassing him if he had to.

Nelson dialed. Four rings. "Hello?" an unfamiliar voice.

"Uh, is Ho...is Nelson there please?"

"Who is this?"

"You don't know me. I'm his brother. We haven't seen each other in decades."

"She bothering you, mister?" Nelson opened one eye. "Because if she's bothering you I can move her over here and come sit next to you," the woman talking through thin lips, pressed thinner to hide bad teeth. Blond hair with black roots, cut to tufts. And enough face jewellery, Nelson guessed, to pay for a capable dentist. "Only I do that I gotta bring the baby with me."

Nelson rolled his opened orb down to find a girl-child in the aisle seat next to him, quietly playing with an armless doll in a blue pinafore. At about six, she looked something like (Nelson guessed again) the woman in the seat across from her had looked maybe fourteen years earlier.

"No. No trouble."

"The baby's too young to sit by herself and Clara is too young to keep an eye on her. Only you look tired is the reason I asked. Very tired. Are you all right, mister?"

"Fine."

"Sure?"

"Sure."

"Because I can come sit next to you if Clara's keeping you from your rest."

Nelson opened the other eye and surveyed the rest of the bus. Maybe he'd been snoring and this was the woman's way of getting him to turn over. But no faces looked back. He checked his watch. He'd had a good hour anyway. Sitting up: "She's fine. I've just come from visiting family myself. Believe me, she's no trouble at all."

His closest living relatives, more than twice the age of this woman, had been more trouble than either of her two children.

"Your father's brother," he'd repeated in the terminal after another voice had come on the phone asking who he was. "Your uncle. We've never met. I haven't seen your father since you were born. I'm at the bus terminal. I've come to see him now."

"I don't know. What's your name?"

"Twiss, just like your old man's. Just like yours, for chrissakes." But not Nelson. That was their father, so they thought. What about Horatio? Had his brother ever had to explain that name to them? "Seymour, only I don't care to use it," realizing he needed to change his tone if he were going to get anywhere with these babies. "The Texas Tornado I was called for a while, then the Massachusetts Mauler. Up north I was the Windsor..." what? Withholder? That wouldn't work. "...Whatchamacallit."

"Windsor..."

"Whatchamacalit." He was stuck with it now.

And they still didn't get it. "What did you say?"

"I was in the wrestles. Black sheep of the family, tell the truth. It's been a knock-about life," Nelson admitted. "I need to see my brother one more time. I mean, what harm can it do?"

More muffled discussion. "Dad's not here. He's in hospital. I'm sorry to tell you, he has cancer."

"All the more reason I should see him, before we're both of us dead, eh?" Nelson caught the draw of breath. "Sorry. You didn't need to hear that. What hospital?"

"Who did you say you were?" It had been like prodding the night-shift gas jockeys back before the war, dumb as sticks the lot of them.

"His brother. Your uncle."

"Wait there. We'll come get you. If you are who you say, Dad'll want to see you, I guess. We'll drive you to the hospital."

Who would claim to be Horatio's brother who wasn't, Nelson wondered. He should have no trouble getting loose of the nephews at the hospital. "I'll be in the diner, wearing a brown overcoat. And a hat. And a walker."

Outside, the terminal was sleek, a deco affair that at one time had suggested movement, going places, until everyone had gone and left this tiered wedding-cake of a building behind.

"A person needs family to count on," the woman on the bus said. "I'm taking the girls to see their gramma now, in East St. Louis." The window seat beyond the woman was piled with over-full, plastic bags and a diaper kit. "Where you headed?"

"Ticket says Chicago. Somebody there I might look up. The Ohio Open Kitchen; ever hear of it? Doesn't matter. I'm prepared for whatever, experienced a change, you see. Reinvigorated. My faith in humanity restored, you might say."

"That's good." The woman smiled, despite her bad teeth. "The girls haven't seen their gramma since Clara was born, have you, Clara?" The little girl ignored her mother, adjusting the dress on her dolly's torso.

"I hadn't seen my brother in fifty years," Nelson said. "You don't want to let it go that long."

"Hello, Horatio," he'd said.

It was another private room like the one in Toronto, this time with Horatio, not Suzette, in the bed, skin tight over his skull, one hand working at the sheets pulled to his neck, eyes peering to the doorway light that silhouetted Nelson. "Who's there? Nobody's called me that in years."

Nelson eased the door to, leaving enough hall-light to see the bed. "It's me, Nelson."

He'd left the nephews in the lobby, surprised how going slow exhausts those accustomed to the world's hurly-burly. Nelson had inched his walker from the bus terminal to the curb where one nephew kept the car idling, the younger man squinting into the big Buick's mirrors to monitor the progress of an approaching metre maid. Nelson timed it so the maid was tapping the car's windshield and pointing out the "No Standing" sign while he scuffled a slow 180 toward the back seat, the nephew gesturing frantically between Nelson and the city official as she got out her ticket pad. Nelson lowered himself into the seat as the maid finished writing.

"This is mighty nice of you," Nelson had said as the almost-a-cop handed the nephew his citation, then, "Wait! Wait!" as the car pulled from the curb. "My walker."

The car jammed into reverse and the other nephew dispatched from the passenger seat to stow Nelson's aid in the trunk. At the other end of their trip, Nelson again shuffled slowly from the hospital parking lot. Before they reached the cancer ward the nephews had been happy to search out cafeteria coffee, leaving Nelson to press on alone toward his brother.

"You're dead, Nelson. You died in the war. I'm Nelson now."

Nelson moved forward. "You think I'm a ghost? Here, feel that," holding forth an arm. "That's real gabardine, that is. You think ghosts wear gabardine?"

"He must have been so happy to see you," the woman on the bus said, tucking her baby up under her raised T-shirt.

In fact Horatio had grasped at the button on the end of a chord that would summon a nurse.

"Well, surprised at least," the bus woman said.

"Surprised to see me?" Nelson had asked Horatio but his brother had shaken his head. "You've been following me all along. I felt you. You were always there, just out of sight. I could never get rid of you."

Quietly, gripping the pistol in his pocket: "You tried. In London."

"You hadn't the sense to stay away from windows while the bombs dropped. I knew, the way you wandered around, sooner or later the Blitz would get you. So it did."

"Know why I'm here?"

Horatio had peered, shaken his head again. "I don't much care. You nearly got me killed in Moose Jaw. I imagine you'd like to forget that. Left me waiting for cops, weren't going to come because you were too scared to take down that gas station."

"I wasn't scared. It just, it wasn't right. It was one thing to play our teachers for fools. Beating up on gas jockeys for spending money, that was something else."

"Not right! You left me in a room full of farm boys with pool cues and reason to use them," Horatio said. "You said you'd do it and I trusted you. They tried to break my wrists, for chrissakes. And then you strut into emergency, with more brass than a marching band, and start right in charming the nurses. You think that was right?"

"You framed us up in Calgary."

"I did. I couldn't stand it, knowing what you had planned at the Palliser for my Suzette. Me still with her touch on my face."

Nelson caught a sudden whiff of sour off the baby, a long rumbling burp having parted her lips. But it was more than that. "Shift over here, Clara," the young mother said, pulling a white cloth from the diaper kit. She flattened out the aisle seat next to Nelson, the man in the seat behind grunting.

Nelson saw Horatio in the hospital, lips curled as he pushed the button on the cord again.

"She loved me," Nelson said.

"She loved me. She only thought she loved you. And I proved it. I went back for her."

"You left me for dead. You wouldn't have had to do that, wouldn't have had to live with my name all these years if it was you she really loved."

"But it was me she slept beside just the same."

"And you've two fools for sons to show for it."

Horatio winced, but Nelson suspected something more than anger driving his brother's white-knuckled grip on the button cord.

Standing in the bus aisle, Clara's mother removed safety pins from the cloth at her baby's waist, pinching them between thin lips. She lifted her infant by the feet, slid out the diaper, folded it over and swiped at the baby's chubby genitals. Then, "Hold this," handing Nelson the soiled white cloth. "You must have had quite a gabfest, you and your brother, after so many years."

A nurse in a blue smock had busied into the hospital room causing Horatio to peel drying lips from his teeth, rasping, "Can I have my shot now? Please?"

The nurse had checked Horatio's chart, taken his wrist in one hand while looking at her watch. "It's too early, hon. Another thirty-five minutes, all right?"

"Please."

"Half an hour. Then I'll be back," moving the cord and button beyond his reach. She had smiled at Nelson and left.

Horatio's clutch went back to his bed covers. His eyes rolled to the ceiling, then squeezed shut as his lips parted hard against his teeth. His body arched. He panted, held his breath, panted again, held, until finally turning toward Nelson watching from the bedside.

"Sixty years since I saw you, nearly. Good years. Say what you have to say and leave me."

Nelson had already relaxed his grip on the pistol. He pushed to a chair, folded his walker into the corner and sat.

"We didn't talk much," Nelson said to the woman on the bus. "It was enough just to be there."

Dead Like Dogs
by William Bankier

Ellery Queen once said, "No one in the business writes about music better than William Bankier." Frequently, Bill's work strikes a chord of darkness. He is fully aware of the poisonous nature of relationships, and the price of suspicion, deceit and greed. His most powerful stories feature characters punished for pursuing their desires. Born in Belleville, Ontario, Bill has lived in Montreal and London and now resides in Los Angeles. A frequent contributor to *Ellery Queen Mystery Magazine* since 1962, Bill has been nominated for both the Arthur Ellis and Edgar Awards. In 1995, a collection of sixteen of his stories was published by Mosaic Press under the title *Fear Is a Killer*.

After a couple of nights bedding down in Hagen's semi-basement in South London, Allan Piper had become accustomed to the big Alsatian, Gringo, sleeping outside the blanket with his jaw resting on Piper's ankle.

Not yet ready to close his eyes, Piper had rummaged on a shelf for something to read, had discovered a Montreal Forum hockey program from a couple of years ago. He was leafing through the pages, staring at action photographs of players who made the game look easy. Piper knew how difficult it could be; he was reduced to trying out for the Streatham Strollers, not even the best team in England.

Turning another page, Piper came to the photograph of goaltender Michel Larocque. Across the page in scrawled handwriting was the pathetic statement: "I have to do it—I'm not as good as you." Ford Hagen must have scribbled this confession. But so what? Not many goalies could kick out the puck as consistently as Larocque.

Piper made an encouraging noise. "Hey, boy," he whispered, not wanting to attract Hagen and Anna from the front room because he had heard enough about how most things in his host's life had turned to rat spit. Maybe after all he would turn down his friend's invitation to play in England. The game wasn't much fun anymore. Maybe he was ready to go back to Baytown.

Responding to Piper's signal, the dog raised his head—a fine grey muzzle, honest eyes. The Alsatian looked at him with such decency, Piper felt the anxiety draining out of him. Dogs had the gift, they lived in a straight line. Judging every moment on its merits, they did not bear grudges or seek revenge. So close to man and yet better than man, wise dependable Gringo deserved to inherit the earth.

Voices murmured down the hall. Ford and Anna were deciding whether or not to watch the late film. Gringo closed his eyes and lowered his head. Cool air filtered in through the mock orange outside the open window.

There were footsteps scraping on the paved area in front of the garage. Somebody came down the concrete steps, slowly. Piper held his breath and listened. Gringo's head came up again.

The front-door buzzer sounded. In the other room, a newspaper was flung aside, Ford Hagen's voice made noises of discontent, his slippers scuffed across the parquet floor.

When he opened the door, things happened quickly. The visitor must have bullied his way inside because Hagen began to complain. Then there was a popping noise—once, twice—and Hagen said no more. Anna screamed until the popping silenced her. With ferocity rumbling in his throat, Gringo had sprung from the bed at first sound of forced entry and now he was in the front room, but the gun—it must have been a silenced gun—popped again and Gringo yelped for the last time.

Piper acted without thinking. As the dog ran from the room, he switched off his light. Now he lay in darkness, both hands covering his face. Don't come in here, he said to himself, and then, to make it more effective, he formed the words with his lips—"God, please don't let him come in here."

The intruder had done most of what he had come to do. But he wasn't finished yet. As Piper listened, he heard slow movements, then a hissing noise, a pause—the hiss again. The sound reminded him of something. It was his father in the garden back home with an aerosol can of insecticide, putting paid to green fly.

The intruder left the apartment, closing the door carefully behind him. Footsteps climbed the outside stairs two at a time. Silence. Piper began to tremble, to feel ashamed. Ford Hagen had taken him into his home, had fed him and advised him. Yet when danger erupted, Piper's only thought was to save himself.

But what could he have done against an armed man? The thought occurred that his friends might be alive, so he hurried down the dark corridor into the front room. The bullet hole in Anna Hagen's head and the pool of blood on the carpet told him she was dead.

But Ford made a sound in his throat. Piper went to him and knelt down. His friend stared up at him with glazed eyes. The wound was in his chest. "What did you say?" Piper asked.

"Said slow," the dying man whispered.

"I know. I was afraid. I'm sorry, Fordie, I didn't see what I could do." But Hagen sighed, closed his eyes, was gone.

Piper, kneeling, looked around the room and saw the normality of it. With the sound turned off, the television screen showed him the titles of the late movie, *The Asphalt Jungle*. Piper was filled with childish protest—he wanted everything to be all right so he could sit and see pathetic old Doc feeding money into the jukebox, watching the young girl dance while all the time the police were closing in on the roadhouse.

No, not everything was normal. He saw the markings on the mirror that had not been there before—a swastika and the letters *NF*. That explained the hissing sound, an aerosol can of paint.

Gringo summoned him with a whimper. He went to the dog and saw the bloody wound in its stomach. The animal didn't know what had happened to him, or why. He was in pain and he wanted his friend Piper to help him.

The memory came back in images clearer than the grey movements on the television screen. Piper and the other kids had stopped playing on a summer morning to watch Nelson Flanagan, who lived in the big house at the end of the lane, bring out his collie dog, Prince, to put him down. The dog was old and sick, hardly able to walk. Nelson put him in a box and closed the lid, hooked up a length of hose to his car exhaust, fed the other end through a hole cut in the box. He switched on the engine and ran it for a while. Then he said, "Prince has gone to sleep."

Nelson Flanagan was always doing memorable things. Once he made a bow out of ironwood and braided cobbler's thread and shot an arrow straight up into the sky, so high it never came down.

First things first. Piper pulled out some clothes, then looked around for a box. He found one in a cupboard, a large carton full of spare bedding. He emptied it, brought it to the front room, lifted Gringo as carefully as possible, and slipped him inside. The dog moaned but looked at him encouragingly.

Hagen's car keys were on a shelf by the front door. Piper put them in his pocket, then lugged the box up the outside stairs and set it down beside the garage door. The hose he found in the garage was too narrow to go over the exhaust pipe but he made it fit by winding it around with masking tape. The other end he thrust through a hole he made in the side of the box.

"Okay, boy," he said brightly, as if they were going for a walk, "soon over!" As he closed the cardboard flaps, he saw liquid eyes looking up at him with approval.

Piper switched on the engine and left it running as he went inside to telephone the police.

The police officers had taken photographs, dusted for prints, and carried away the bodies, including that of the dog. The inspector had been casting glances at Piper since his admission that he had taken time to put Gringo to sleep before dialling 999. "We might have had a chance of catching him."

"How? He was up the stairs and gone. After I dialled, it took you twenty minutes. He'd have been miles away."

"Even so." The inspector did not appreciate people stonewalling him with logic.

Piper remembered Hagen's dying words and decided to offer them up even though they made him look bad. Having explained how he had switched off the light and hidden in the back room while his friends were murdered, he had been dealt another of the policeman's scornful stares. Now he admitted, "Hagen spoke to me just before he died. 'Said slow.' "

"Said slow?"

"I guess he meant I was slow in getting to him."

"You didn't exactly go charging into the breach."

Alone again, Piper could think of nothing to do but have the sleep he was missing. The police had warned him to touch nothing in the living room, they might want to go over it again. They took the front door key so when he let himself out it would be forever.

"What about the marks on the mirror?" he asked the departing inspector.

"National Front? They sometimes kill people. Were your friends anti-fascists?"

"Not that I was aware."

"We'll check it."

Piper moved his things to a furnished room, asking himself as he paid a week in advance why he was not on an airplane flying home. He wasn't interested in laying for the Streatham Strollers now, even if they'd have him, which was no sure thing. Ford Hagen as goaltender and respected member of the team had promised to recommend him. Now Ford was gone and maybe he should go, too.

Instead, he sat in a chair in a room with sad wallpaper drinking tins of beer and watching daytime television, that glossy English picture looking smooth as an oil painting. They had their silly game shows but the big difference was no commercials on two of the channels. Also, many of the faces had bad teeth.

As he wasted a couple of days this way, not shaving, mildly in shock, waiting for the inspector to ring and announce that he had arrested a maniac with National Front sympathies, Piper's mind turned constantly to the dying dog. Not his friend Ford, or Annie the innocent wife, but brave Gringo, racing to his master's assistance regardless of danger to himself. After it was all over, Hagen had blamed him for being slow. But that loyal dog saw him only as a friend who was able to put him out of his misery.

A news program came on the box. They worked through the current crop of work stoppages and factory closures, then got down to the local stories. Ford Hagen's name was mentioned, then up came the face of the man who owned the hockey team—wealthy businessman, owner of a thriving automobile dealership, head of the South London Commercial Association, Mr. Cedric Sloane.

As Sloane was interviewed, expressing his shock at the loss of his imported goaltender, Piper decided he would not like to buy a car, new or used, from this man. Broad-faced, russet-skinned, pale eyes wide behind rimless glasses, the man exuded a farmer sincerity that rang as true as a plastic wine glass. But it was the friendly form of address used over and over again by the announcer that began to get through to Piper. He heard it as, "Said...said...said..." but realized in the end that it was an abbreviation of Cedric. At the close of the interview, the broadcaster turned to the camera: "That was Ced Sloane, owner of the Streatham Strollers, who this week lost his all-star goal-minder."

Ced Sloane. Said slow.

Piper snapped open another tin of beer and weighed the possibilities. Was it characteristic of Ford Hagen to needle a good friend with his dying words? Or was it more likely that he offered the name of his killer, Ced Sloane. Not that the sanctimonious tycoon was in the apartment that night pulling the trigger. He would have paid somebody to do his killing.

Piper decided not to telephone the police station. More than likely the detective would attend the funeral, scanning the faces of mourners for a sort of involuntary police lineup. Next morning, shaved and dressed in his good suit, he went to the chapel where the service was being held. Hagen had played so many seasons in England, he had more friends here than back in Canada. His coffin and Annie's were lined up on the track, ready to roll through the curtain to the furnace.

The inspector was in the crowd. When the last prayer was said, Piper got out fast and waited on the pavement in unexpected sunshine. "I have a new lead," he said when the policeman joined him.

"I spoke to a man at the National Front," the inspector said. "This was nothing to do with them, they're using all their resources to hassle Asians in the East End. The killer must have thought he could send us down the wrong road."

Piper shook his head. "It occurred to me when I saw him on television. Cedric Sloane. Ford wasn't telling me I was slow just before he died. He was giving me a name. Ced Sloane."

The inspector stared at Piper as if his eyes were printing the stockmarket prices. "Sloane owns the hockey team. Hagen was his goalminder. You're telling me he had him killed?"

"Why don't you ask him?"

"He's one of the leading figures in South London. Why don't I ask you? We have only your word there was an intruder."

"Do you believe I shot my friend and his wife and their dog?"

"No. And I won't believe Cedric Sloane was behind it until you show me motive." The inspector moved away. Then he came back to drive the final nail into the box holding Piper's supposition. "Sloane is on Her Majesty's next Honours List. He's going to be Sir Cedric."

"And I shall be the Queen of the May," Piper murmured, but not until the officer was out of earshot.

Piper decided he could not leave England without having a word with Cedric Sloane. He took a taxi to Wimbledon and climbed out in front of the glass facade of Sloane Motor Sales, which occupied almost an entire block on the Broadway not far from the town hall. He went inside and asked the receptionist if he could see the boss. Letting his Canadian accent hang out, he told her he was a friend of the late Ford Hagen, a fellow hockey player.

She was a big blond, with short hair brushed forward around a boyish face with level blue eyes. When she left the desk and walked away, Piper watched her rangy legs and found himself wishing it was a long walk. She returned from the inner office and said, "He's busy but he can spare you five minutes."

The television camera hadn't lied about anything except stature. Sloane was bereft of sincerity but he was shorter than he had appeared on screen.

"Thank you for seeing me, sir," Piper said. "There's something I have to ask you."

"You must be the defenceman Ford was telling me about. If you're half the player he said, there's a place for you with the Strollers."

"It has to do with Ford. I was with him when he died."

The businessman looked surprised. "I understood they were alone."

"I was asleep in the back room." This was the lie Piper was telling to justify his avoidance of trouble. "I heard the shots. By the time I could get to the front room, the killer was gone. But Ford was still alive. And he told me something."

"This is news to me."

"He said your name. His dying words were, 'Ced Sloane.'"

Sloane waited. "Well?"

"Why did he mention your name?"

"Don't ask me. Maybe he wanted you to come to me about playing hockey."

"I don't think it was that vague. When a man is dying, he says something important. In this case, I think he was telling me the identity of the man behind the murder."

"Where is your proof?"

"I haven't any. It's just a hunch." Piper stared at Sloane. "But there's the way you've started talking louder."

Sloane's face darkened. "You don't *know* how loud I can talk," he thundered. "My voice carries a long way in this part of the world." He controlled himself with difficulty. "And you, my boy, can forget about playing ice hockey anywhere in England."

"It's the motive that's got me baffled. The inspector asked me, where's the motive?"

"You've told this rubbish to the police?"

Piper nodded. "Waste of time. Your cops are even more establishment-oriented than the ones back home. Never criticize a pillar of the community, it isn't done, old boy. It's not on."

"Let me complete your education," Sloane said. "If you spread this story anywhere else, you'll find yourself in court facing a suit for slander."

Piper retreated from the inner office. He felt humiliated, controlled. The ancient Greeks must have experienced the same feeling of insignificance when their gods had finished knocking them about. He was heading for the street door when the receptionist came after him.

"What was the explosion in there?"

"Mr. Sloane doesn't like me."

"He's that way with a lot of people." She looked him in the eye. "What's your crime?"

"Not mine, his." Piper took a chance and told her part of his suspicions. "I don't believe Sloane was at the scene," he concluded, "but he made it happen."

She checked her watch against the wall clock. "It's my lunch break. Can we talk?"

"My pleasure."

She used the intercom to advise her boss that she would be away for an hour. Then she grabbed her handbag and hurried after Piper with the athletic stride of a girl on a playground. "By the way," she said, "I'm Karen Martingale." She gave Piper a hand that was connected to an inner power source. The jolt got his motor started and the hockey player suddenly remembered what fun it is to be alive.

They lunched on shepherd's pie at a pub called The Prince of Wales. Piper drank lager, Karen white wine. The place was nicely crowded, a hundred subdued conversations combining to produce a pleasant buzz. Kids shot pool on a toy table at the back. At the other end, near the bar, men and women paid attention to horse racing on the telly—the only reason why a lot of English people bothered to get out of bed in the morning, as far as Piper could tell.

After some small talk, Piper restated his theory regarding the double murder based on the dying man's last words which he now took to have been "Ced Sloane." A serious mood froze the girl's fork halfway to her mouth. "It fits together," she said.

"What does?"

"A couple of weeks ago, Cedric and I were going to lunch. We stopped off at the bank and he went in to get something from his safety-deposit box. He came back with a thick brown envelope."

"Could have been money."

"Then we made one more stop, at a place called the Aston Recreation Club near Tooting High Street. Cedric went in carrying the envelope and came back without it."

"It means only one thing to me," Piper said.

"Should we go to the police?"

"I've lost my faith in your police."

"Then we do nothing?"

"*I* do something. Fortunately, I have a return ticket to Montreal. I think I'll fly back and report to the Verdun Shamrocks training camp. I'd better make some money."

The girl looked wistful. There was something about the woman's body, the boyish face that reached Piper on a subtle level. "I'd love to see Montreal," she said. "There's no use quitting Sloane and trying to work some other place around here. He'll come and get me."

"Then come with me. I'm sorry, you'll have to buy your own ticket."

"I've got a couple of thousand saved." She gave him a conspiratorial grin. "I can probably help you with the rent."

Another idea began climbing up out of the pool in Piper's mind where the self-destructive urge was suspended in acid. "There's something I want to try before we leave town," he said.

They needed an envelope, so they stopped at a stationery store and bought a few of the kind Sloane had used on the day he made his collection from the safety-deposit box. Sitting in Karen's car, Piper printed a message on a sheet of paper. Before folding it and sealing it inside an envelope, he showed it to the girl at the wheel. "Any man who would shoot a dog," it read, "is not fit to walk the streets."

As Piper licked the gummed flap, Karen said, "If Sloane's transaction was innocent, the bloke who reads this will wonder if the world has gone mad."

The Aston Recreation Club displayed a brightly painted frontage halfway down a row of decaying terraced houses. "Wait for me," Piper said as he got out of the car.

"Shouldn't I come with you?"

"Keep the engine running."

He went inside and found himself in a low-ceilinged room, with a dozen snooker tables floating in darkness, each within its shaded glow like so many phosphorescent life forms at five hundred fathoms. On a dais near the back, men sat around a table frowning at fists full of cards. There was a bar on one side with shelves of bottles and a couple of pump handles for drawing beer. The man at the bar was working with glue and sandpaper, fitting a new tip to a billiard cue.

Piper approached with a confident stride and slapped the envelope on the bar. "When Ced Sloane was in here a couple of weeks ago—"

"Sir?" The man kept sanding but he was listening.

"The envelope was light. He wants this to go to the bloke concerned."

"It shall be done."

The barman called across the room to the card players. "Eddie?" Nobody moved. "Eddie Poole. You're wanted."

A slab of darkness shifted and moved into the light. The kibitzer, Eddie Poole, shambled forward, wearing a one-piece mechanic's suit without a trace of grease on it. "You called? The head on Poole's shoulders was pale white, vaguely pointed at the top, and it produced an oily glow.

"This is for you," the barman said, pushing the envelope across the mahogany.

"Special delivery from Ced Sloane," Piper added.

Poole picked up the envelope, held it beside his head, listened to it as if I was a cigar. "Who are *you*?"

"Just doing a friend a favour."

"American?"

"The top end," Piper said. "Up where the map goes red." Then he left the recreation club quickly, reasoning that Poole's recreation, when he opened the envelope, might consist of making boot holes in Piper's ribs.

Karen got her car off the side road and into traffic before she said, "What do you think?"

"The man's name is Eddie Poole. Whether he did it or not, he looks capable." Piper gave his instinct a chance to be heard. "He did it."

"Shouldn't you tell the police?"

"A waste of ten pence," Piper said, "assuming we could find a telephone that works."

"There's a phone in my bedroom," she said. "I hate to see you frustrated like this."

The detective-inspector said everything Piper expected him to say. The evidence was circumstantial. Yes, they knew about Eddie Poole, a small-time local gambler. But how could they prove the envelope from Sloane contained money? It could have been accounts receivable—maybe Sloane had debts that needed collecting. Anyway, nobody could stand up in court and say Poole had taken money from Sloane to kill Ford Hagen.

Piper put the telephone back on the bedside table. Karen was sitting beside him with her knees together and her hands in her lap. It was such a domestic setting, they might have been about to compose a grocery list for the weekend. Karen's thoughts seemed to be running parallel to his. She said, "Have you ever been married, Allan?"

"Nobody ever asked me," he said, reaching nervously for a flimsy joke to keep the scene from becoming serious. He was back in Baytown riding in a taxi late at night, coming home from a farmhouse on the edge of town with the inside of his mouth raw from kissing. He was seventeen years old, it was early winter, and the propane heater which would explode and burn the house with everybody in it was a couple of hours away from going off. Connie must have been brushing her teeth, smiling vacantly at herself in the mirror, not bothered any more about the lovemaking, knowing that come June she would be married to Allan Piper, the pretty good young hockey player.

Karen put an arm around his shoulder, drew him gently back to the present. "Don't look so sad," she said. "I only wanted to know if I was with somebody else's man."

"You're with nobody's man," he said. "Not even my own."

An hour later, he was falling asleep beside this girl in the middle of a lazy London summer afternoon. If he could keep this up, life might be worth another try.

Piper had been back in Montreal for so long that he had stopped picking up the London papers at the International News. What was the use? Not a word was going down about anybody helping police with their inquiries into the murder of Ford and Anna Hagen. And gentle, noble Gringo. The file was closed and Cedric Sloane was selling cars from his Wimbledon showroom—maybe buying and selling lives, too, if anybody else was getting in his way.

It was late October and the first snow was falling on Montreal. Winter was back early, eager to take possession again after a short absence. Karen was waiting for Piper after the team finished practising. She refused to hang around in the chilly arena but was crouched over a cognac in the brasserie across the street. When she saw her man come in, she raised her chin to the waiter and two foaming glasses of draft beer were on the table by the time Piper had slung his coat on a nail.

"How did it go?"

"Not bad." He was a few pounds lighter than he had been in London, a notch or two tighter. "We should be ready for Chicoutimi when they show on Saturday."

After the practice and the beer, he was hungry. They ordered steaks and salads. Eating in silence, he provoked her into saying, "You can't get it out of your mind."

"More than anything it's the dog," he admitted. "Just before the shooting started, he was lying at the end of my bed. Those eyes." Piper set knife and fork across unwanted food. "He looked at me as if the world was never going to end. Then that bastard Poole broke in."

"If it was Poole."

"It was him. I know it but I can't prove it."

"You don't even have a motive. You say Ced Sloane hired Poole to do the killing. Why?"

"I've been thinking about that," Piper reached into his back pocket and drew out a tattered magazine. He handed it to Karen who turned a few pages.

"A hockey program for a Canadiens' game," she said.

"I found it in Hagen's apartment. Here, let me find you the page." He leafed through and found the photo of goaltender Larocque with the handwriting across it. "Ford must have written that."

Karen read aloud. "I have to do it—I'm not as good as you." She turned the program over as if looking for an answer. "What does it mean?"

"What if Hagen was involved in throwing the occasional game? Letting in a goal or two so the Strollers would lose when they were expected to win."

"Sloane gambles," Karen confirmed.

"Ford was doing this so Sloane could profit. Taking money to throw games." Piper looked again at the tortured handwriting. "He hated himself for doing it. And one day he was looking at this picture of Larocque, a guy who bleeds whenever a puck goes past him. Maybe he was drunk. Full of self-pity. So he wrote this justification."

"It may be true. But why would Sloane have him killed?"

"That's easy," Piper said. "Hagen was going to blow the whistle. Confess publicly."

Two inches of snow lay on the car's windshield when they came out of the brasserie. Piper brushed off the front, Karen did the back, then they got in and drove away. "Autumn in Montreal," he muttered as packed snow groaned under the tires.

"When are you going to forget this?" Karen said.

"When I get to the bottom of it."

"This isn't what I wanted."

"What do you want?"

"Happiness."

"Too much unfinished business," Piper said grimly.

The telephone rang in the night. Karen answered and Piper lay half awake, listening. "This is a crazy time to call. Are you drunk? No, I'm not coming back, I think I like it better here." She sounded coy. "Do what you like," she concluded. "I can't stop you."

Piper hoisted himself onto one elbow, reached across Karen and took the telephone from her. The voice mumbling on the overseas line was the one he expected to hear. "Mr. Sloane," he said, "this is Allan Piper."

"The two of you together in the middle of the night," Sloane said. "Now I get the picture."

"You had Ford Hagen killed and you got away with it. Now here you are sniffing around where you can only make more trouble."

"Persuade Karen to come back to London. Or I'll show you what trouble can be."

"How does it feel to be above the law?"

"I won't wait forever."

The telephone went down at the other end. Piper replaced his bedside receiver in the cradle. Then Karen opened her arms and accepted him against the warmth of her body. He relaxed and floated in a pocket of invulnerability. This was not sex, it was reassurance—and Piper decided that the saddest thing in the world is somebody sleeping alone.

The idea of holding a Ford Hagen Memorial Game emerged around that time—the only question was why nobody had thought of it sooner. It meant a sellout on a night when the rink would otherwise have been dark. The Shamrocks all wore black arm bands. The opposition was a team of all-stars, including Verdun old-timers and a couple of local lads who made it to the big league with the Islanders and the Nordiques.

Piper felt strange staring at the blue line with his head bowed during the silence in memory of Hagen. Knowing what he knew, it seemed improper that the business should remain unfinished. And having failed Hagen on the big night, what right had Allan Piper to be out here on the ice paying tribute? At the very least, he ought to start the game in the penalty box.

The first period was almost over when he saw Cedric Sloane and Eddie Poole in their rink-side seats. They looked more prosperous than the hockey fans around them. While he was on the bench between shifts, Piper couldn't keep his eyes off them. Even when he was on the ice, he felt his attention divided between the game and the English visitors. He caught sight of Karen in her seat halfway up the stands. Had she seen them yet?

When play ended after the first twenty minutes, Piper skated over to the boards and spoke to Sloane. "Nice of you to come all this way," he said. "Hagen would be pleased."

"The game is only a sidelight," Sloane said. "We're here to collect Karen and take her back home."

"That won't work. Unless you've added kidnapping to your list of activities."

"Clever bastard," Poole said. He took hold of the player's sweater.

Sloane knocked his hand away. "Are you crazy?"

"We all know the answer to that one," Piper said. As he started to skate away, Sloane spoke to him seriously.

"By the way, is this your best game, Piper? If it is, I'm afraid you'd never have won a place on my team."

During the third period, Piper was on the bench again, replaced by one of the younger players. He cared, but not very much. He noticed the two rinkside seats were empty. Glancing up at Karen's place, he saw that she had left the arena, too. An uneasy feeling cramped his gut. He wondered what the coach would say if he left the bench and got changed. It wouldn't go down well—he was barely holding onto his job with the team as it was.

Showered and changed, he got into his car and drove home. The night was frosty clear. He rolled into the lane beside the building, unlocked his garage, and parked the car inside.

Upstairs, Karen was in the bedroom, her suitcase open on the bed. "Whatever else they say about Ced Sloane," Piper said from the doorway, "the man sure can sell."

"This is better for everybody, Allan."

"A hell of a lot better for Karen Martingale."

She paused in her movements between wardrobe and suitcase. She came to him. "In London, I really believed this was what I wanted. For the first few weeks here, I thought the same. I've never lied to you."

"The other night in bed, I lay in your arms and I thought I could be all right."

"We're good together in a lot of ways. But there's more to getting through life. Every day has twenty-four hours in it." She returned to her packing. "I have to see to my future."

"And Allan Piper doesn't have any."

"The way things are, you're a hockey player at the end of his career. You have nothing after you retire. What do you intend to do?"

"They always need somebody to sweep the rink."

"That's just what I mean." Her suitcase closed and that abrupt thud was the last sound between them for a while.

Later, in the kitchen, she found him having a drink. He offered to pour one for her but she refused.

"Are they coming to pick you up?"

She glanced at her watch. "In a few minutes."

Piper quoted a song that was popular when he was young and before Karen was born. "So long," he said, "it's been good to know ya."

His mind was made up from the time the front doorbell rang. "Do me a favour," he said, offering her a ten-dollar bill. "I'm going to need a bottle of whisky."

"Can't you go?"

"I'm half dressed. Will you do this one thing for me?"

She took the money, their relationship having deteriorated into that of a sullen child with her troublesome father. She passed Sloane and Poole at the door. "Back soon," she said as she headed for the street.

"How are we for hard feelings?" Sloane said, entering the kitchen.

"None whatever. Have a drink."

"It's a pity," Poole said. "I'm good at sorting out hard feelings." He sat at the table.

"Take a look at him, Eddie," Sloane said. "You can always spot the athlete over the hill. He becomes a loser."

Piper had poured three drinks and now he handed them around. "I'm backing off," he said, "because it's better for Karen without me around."

"Karen knows her place," Sloane said. He raised his glass. "Good health."

"Long life." Piper drank. "Something you should see," he said. He took Sloane by the arm and led him out of the kitchen. "An old photograph of Ford Hagen as a lad." In the living room, he bent to retrieve an album. "Would you switch on that light?"

As Sloane turned to fumble with the lamp switch, Piper rose with a lead doorstop in his hand, raised it, and brought it down across the Englishman's head, caught him as he fell and lowered the unconscious body onto the settee.

"Poole!" he called "Could you come in here?" Then he stood beside the doorway, the weight in his hand. As Eddie came into the room, Piper swung sidearm and took him across the forehead. He made no attempt to catch him as he fell.

Now he had to hurry. Karen would be back in a few minutes. Hoisting Sloane in a fireman's lift, he carried him down the stairs, out the door, and along the lane to the garage. He managed to open the door, lug Sloane inside, and sling him across the back seat. Then he hurried back for Poole and brought him downstairs to join his unconscious boss inside the car.

Piper made one last trip upstairs to write the note. He scribbled quickly on the pad they used for grocery lists, tore off the page, and left it on the kitchen table.

> *Karen,*
> *I've gone and taken Sloane and Poole with me. Don't try to follow. Go back to London and forget you ever knew any of us.*
> *Love, if that's what it was,*
Allan

He left the front door of the apartment on the latch so she could get in. Then he went inside the garage and closed the door. It was dark—he had to feel his way, hands on freezing metal, to get inside and behind the wheel. When he switched it on, the dash lighted up to keep him company.

There was plenty of gas in the tank, the motor would idle for a long time. Longer than would be needed. The stunned men in the back seat lay without moving. Piper folded his arms and closed his eyes. He smelled frosty air and the pungent odour of exhaust fumes. Minute followed minute on the face of the dashboard clock.

Nelson Flanagan came out into the lane carrying old Prince in his arms and lowered him gently into the cardboard box. The kids held back, aware of what an important thing was happening that day.

Gringo raised his head from Piper's lap and gave him a look that said there was nothing to be afraid of. Piper slept.

Crocodile Tears
by Leslie Watts

You might not think that the illustrator of books like *The Most Beautiful Kite in the World* and *You Can't Rush a Cat* would understand the noirish nether-worlds of hatred and vengeance. But Leslie Watts proves that calm surfaces can be deceiving. Leslie has illustrated ten children's books for other authors, plus two of her own stories, *The Troll of Sora* and *Princess Stinky-Toes and the Brave Frog Robert*. Her adult crime novel *The Chocolate Box* was published in 1991 and was a finalist for both the Arthur Ellis and Anthony Awards. Leslie also writes for the acclaimed CTV drama series *The Eleventh Hour*.

I ask for the smoking section. I've heard that Jonathan hasn't been able to give up the Gitanes, even after the spot showed up on the X-ray. I order a soda with lime and a dozen oysters and sit waiting.

I was twenty-four in 1978 when I married Jonathan Raffe. He was fifty-two. We met at the audition for *Rising up to Heaven*. I'd seen all seven of the films he'd directed, from *Linehan's Folly* to *Roses, Bloody Roses*—though I'd had to borrow my sister's ID to get into *The Trouble with Snakes*—and I knew that if I got the part in *Heaven* my career would be assured. I wasn't a great actress—I probably wasn't even good—but Donald Kelleher, my agent, called me the morning I boarded the plane to London and said, "Short skirt, high heels, tight sweater." Donald knew his mark. I got the lead. Three weeks into the shoot, Jonathan and I were in bed together and he was sketching out plans for his second divorce.

We bought a flat north of Kensington Gardens and made four more films together. *Still Waters*, which followed *Heaven*, mystified critics who were not used to panning a Raffe film; they were generous if cautious. The next two were utter failures. The production company lost money in both instances, and it was suggested by several people in the know that Jonathan's career was over. Then, one night in Cannes, we read the script for *Lion Hunt* by a young writer named Alan Karkov. Before I was halfway through it, I told Jonathan that I'd been born for the part of Alicia Cameron. When you are twenty-eight, you still believe that a lie is a fine sacrifice to make if it will change the fortune of the one you love.

Back then Karkov was unknown. Now, of course, he's gone Hollywood and no one can have him for less than a million five. But in 1982, with a mere six hundred pounds on the option, it seemed that I might actually summon the power to resuscitate my husband's career. When you are twenty-eight, such things seem possible. The largest consequences can spring from the smallest acts, and an entire life can be rebuilt on a single success. When you are twenty-eight, you believe that six hundred pounds can turn a life around.

The waiter brings my oysters and soda, and when he retreats, Jonathan is standing in his wake. He has not changed much. Perhaps he is smaller, although it's hard to be sure. I find I often conjure up my friends in sizes that are at odds with reality, and it's possible that I do the same with those for whom I feel nothing but indifference. What remains of his hair is a grey fringe that grazes the top of his pilled wool turtleneck. His uniform has not changed much either. He is rich; he looks poor. His dark cotton pants could use a good swish through a heavy duty cycle. I stand to kiss his unshaven cheeks. He puts a hand on my waist, though it begins to creep up almost immediately, and, with the second kiss, comes to rest on the side of my left breast.

"Yes," I tell him, "they're still there."

His lips are thinner and when he grins they nearly disappear. There's one change: his teeth have been capped. He sits across from me, ankle over knee, and looks me in the eye. "How are you, Gillian?" he says. "You look marvellous. It's all right to smoke in here, I suppose. Toronto not gone all mad yet? You do look marvellous, darling. Really, you do. I didn't know what to expect, of course. One never does these days. Thought you might have gone in for all that nip-and-tuck nonsense. Why do women do it? Really, why do they?"

"Maybe," I say, borrowing an ashtray from the neighbouring table, "because their husbands are always divorcing them for twenty-year-old girls."

"Well, that's a point, of course."

"Though why their wives would want to stop them, I'll never understand."

"Ah." He draws on his cigarette and gazes around the restaurant. "Anyone here I'd know?"

"Jonathan," I say, "you're in Toronto."

"That's all right." He winks. "I know you. How's old what's-his-name?"

"Patrick," I say evenly. "He's well, thank you."

"Terrific," says Jonathan. "Daughter? Suppose she has children herself."

"Not yet. She's young. Can I get you a drink? Something to eat?"

I signal the waiter and Jonathan orders a large gin and a dozen oysters for himself.

"What about you?" he asks. "Your work."

"I sold the business two years ago."

"Really! Make a lot of money?"

"No," I lie. "It was a bad time for it, but I was ready to get out."

He musters a sympathetic expression. "Of course. Damned stressful, I imagine." There's a small pause as he lights a second cigarette from the butt of the first. "That sort of business."

I see his trouble. "Public relations," I remind him.

"Of course. Marvellous." He chuckles. "Though not much room for artistic expression, I suppose."

"How's yours these days?"

"Oh. I've got my hand in a few things. BBC special, that sort of thing. They interviewed me for the James Thomas bio, did you see it?"

I shake my head.

"Rather embarrassing, actually. Asked me all sorts of questions about those scenes from *Snakes* I'd rather not have answered. But you know how it is." He laughs drily. "I could have used someone like you there. Bit of the old PR, hmm?"

"I imagine you handled it."

For the few moments while we eat our oysters, the silence is almost convivial. Suddenly he says, "I'm going to be seventy-seven, Gillian."

"I know."

"It's not the age I mind. It's the friends. They're all dying."

It is impossible not to laugh. "Jonathan, you know damn well you're living with a woman who's five years younger than I am."

"Jealous?"

"Oh, for Christ's sake. Is that what you're doing here? You're not going to tell me you're dying too."

His oyster shells lie empty. He leans over them. There's a drop of brine on his chin. "You remember Tilly?"

My glass is suddenly empty, but the waiter is nowhere to be seen.

"Tilly Reardon," says Jonathan. "Before that, Tilly Bromley, née Tilson."

I spot the waiter, raise my hand and make eye contact as I ask

Jonathan, "What about her?"

"She's one of the friends," he says, "who have recently died."

I turn to face him. I'm about to tell him that I'm sorry when the waiter arrives. I order a gin and tonic.

"That's the trouble with oysters," says Jonathan. "They make one so thirsty."

He watches me while I wait for the drink. I'm calculating. She couldn't have been more than fifty-five. I don't like to think about people dying young, even middle-aged. Early death in others suggests that my own demise may not be far ahead. I swallow half the drink before he speaks again.

"I met her when Tilson was writing the score for *Linehan's Folly*. He took a crack at *Roses* too, but he had a falling out with Malcolm Packett and ended up being replaced by that damned Sutherland chap—what was his name? It doesn't matter. Anyway, Tilson died shortly after that. Pancreatic cancer. Tilly was devastated. She hadn't lived with her mother for years. I'm sure that's why she leapt headfirst into Bromley's arms. She was only nineteen. Don't look at me like that, darling. I know what you're thinking. But five years is a lot of time at that age. And you were a different sort of person when I met you. Tilly was so...innocent. Tilson would have put an end to it, of course, if he'd lived, but the rest of us had no clout. She was hell-bent on marriage and there was nothing for it. This was all before your time, of course. You were still a schoolgirl in B—oh, hell, darling, I can never remember the name of that place. But that is all by the way. By the time we started shooting *Lion Hunt*, Bromley'd won his BAFTA for *Rigmarole* and Tilly was pregnant with their third child. You'd think she'd have put up a stink about his going halfway around the world to shoot a film, but no, Tilly wasn't like that. Of course, you must have considered all of this over the years, darling, hmm?"

"Yes," I say. My drink is gone. I order another.

"Tilly," says Jonathan, "said goodbye to David Bromley, and everyone knows what happened next."

From the start, the shoot was a nightmare. Generators failed; tents leaked. Most of the British crew seemed to fall almost instantly ill with diseases whose names I hadn't heard since grade-five geography and a doctor had to be flown in during the second week from Dar es Salaam. Silvia Gunn, one of the supporting actresses, broke her ankle two days into filming and had to be replaced by Nora Hatchwell who was even less competent than I was. James Shephard, my co-star, was in the throes of a breakup with his long-time lover and spent his down time drinking bizarre cocktails and begging prescription drugs from the doctor from Dar and, when that ploy failed, from Hair and Wardrobe. When the schedule fell behind by eight days, the African crew left anyway for a previously arranged job, a documentary for Australian television on waterfowl in the Selous Game Reserve. The British and American co-producers spent hours screaming down the phones. The Germans were more efficient; they flew in from Munich and administered their screaming in person, while Peter Kant, the producer, scrambled to find a replacement crew and advised massive script changes. At night, Jonathan wandered the camp, arguing over the next day's schedule with whomever would listen and I became increasingly concerned that he was losing his grip. During the day, unless I had a scene to play, I tried to steer a clear path away from him. I didn't object when, one evening, he dragged his cot to the other side of the tent so that he wouldn't disturb me when he came in hours after I'd fallen asleep. David Bromley, who had been Director of Photography in Africa on both a documentary about crocodiles for the naturalist Wilhelm Burger and a Hollywood feature, seemed the only calm person on the set.

"I warned them in January," he told me after one late dinner. We were walking away from the dining tent, and we carried our folding chairs with us. "Twenty-four days was wildly optimistic. At this time of year in particular. No one listens to the camera man. Except, of course, when it comes to advice about dealing with the local fauna."

I stopped and put my chair down. "That's hardly Jonathan's fault."

He laughed. "No need to be so indignant. I wasn't blaming him." He unfolded his chair, then sat down and lit a cigarette. "Want one?"

"No."

"Sit down," he said. "What are you so cross about anyway? It's not your money."

I hated folding chairs. I never could figure them out.

"Ah," he said as he fixed mine for me, "so it's not the second honeymoon you envisaged."

"Oh, shut up."

He laughed again, though not so loudly as before. "I warned him about that too."

"What do you mean?"

"Why do you suppose Tilly always stays at home? You can't save a marriage by making a film together."

"That's nice," I said sullenly. "I suppose that's the latest rumour. Our marriage on the rocks. It figures."

He said nothing but smoked and looked into the distance where birds sailed above the darkening horizon and something hunched and four-legged moved below.

"Anyway," I said, pulling at my sweater, "I thought Africa was hot all the time." I don't know why I said that. I'd known perfectly well what to expect from the climate. I suppose I wanted to finish the subject of my marriage without having to get up and walk away.

David exhaled and gave me a long look. "Can't you do any better than that?"

I was no good at subtle veering—not back then, at least—and I didn't bother pretending not to understand. "All right," I said, "give me one of your damned cigarettes."

"There's only one real problem with getting behind at this time of year," he said as he flicked his lighter. "I believe it's going to rain."

Alan Karkov flew in the next morning. He spent most of his time in a small tent with Peter Kant at his back and a portable typewriter on his knees. Rain dripped through the canvas and wilted the pages even before they reached Peter's hands. Jonathan sulked behind the wheel of his Land Rover, reading the revisions through a cigarette fog, and I huddled miserably on my sodden cot, watching mosquitoes hurl themselves against the stained netting and thinking that perhaps James was right to drink himself into a stupor before noon. That week we shot only nine scenes, and it was nearly impossible to find a member of the cast or crew who could speak a full sentence without shouting or bursting into tears. The Germans went back to Munich in disgust and Peter Kant threatened to cut his losses and close the whole thing down if something positive didn't happen fast. It was David who suggested that we move down river where the canopy of trees would check the worst of the rain. He spent nearly an hour in muted conversation with a young Tanzanian named Matthew before inviting Alan, Jonathan and Peter to join them in his tent. When they emerged, the half-crew that Peter Kant had managed to cobble together in place of the African defectors was ordered to move the set two miles north before nightfall.

We drove along a muddy track to the location that Matthew had recommended, and in an area more sheltered than our previous camp, we set about putting up the tents and arranging our gear. By dusk, a generator had grudgingly roused itself, so lights were beginning to come on as Matthew walked Jonathan and me around the site. "Not a big river," he said. "But it is just the thing, don't you think? A bridge is farther along, down that way. And in that way, another, but not so good. At this time of year…" He shrugged.

"A vehicular bridge?" asked Jonathan.

Matthew smiled. "Oh, not that sort of bridge. This is a foot bridge only, quite narrow. You can walk only, maybe carry a few things, but nothing too big. No vehicles for sure. I will get more men to carry what you need. There are such men nearby."

Jonathan said that he understood and, as he turned away from Matthew and surveyed the new situation, I saw him smile for the first time in days. "It's terrific," he said. "We'll use the water in the second act for the tryst."

Matthew had been walking away, but now he turned back, a look of consternation on his face. "Please do not go into the water. It is not safe. There are crocodiles."

"Of course," said Jonathan. "Mere background is all we need. A little scenery to set the tone."

That night we resumed shooting and for the next few days James Shephard stayed sober enough to remember most of his lines and Alan Karkov learned to hold his tongue when he didn't. Jonathan's mood continued to improve, and the night before the final disaster I went to thank David in his tent.

"Don't be ridiculous," he said. He'd been lying on his cot, reading by the light of a lantern, and now he stubbed out his cigarette and closed his book. "I was being entirely selfish. I don't like it when jobs suddenly go away." He sat up and looked at me curiously. "What about you? I had the impression you were ready to pack it in. I hope you weren't disappointed we stayed on."

"Disappointed! Jonathan would have been impossible to live with if we'd had to quit."

He said, "Hmm," and I felt suddenly embarrassed. "Drink?" he offered. "I have a bottle of something here. Don't tell James. I'm trying to make it last."

I laughed.

"You know," he said as we tapped our paper cups together, "the age difference only matters when it's bad. Tilly's twelve years younger than I am. She only minds when she's pissed off at me. The rest of the time I think she rather enjoys it."

"Thank you, David," I said. "You're very kind." I swallowed my drink and embraced him.

"I am not kind," he said, squeezing my arm. "I am honest. I am rational. If you're going to stay for another drink, then please close the zip. I do not wish to be eaten alive."

Jonathan says, "I wonder how the main dishes are."

"Expensive," I tell him.

"Great. What will you have?"

"Nothing. Thank you."

"The way you're knocking back that gin, you'd better have something."

He orders a steak and salad for himself and a plate of gnocchi for me. I'm beginning to poke at it before he takes up his story again.

"You remember Matthew?" he asks. "The guide? I went back to see him. In April. I was in Kenya, visiting old friends who retired there, and I thought it would be good fun to cross into Tanzania and look him up."

I put down my fork. "You what?"

"We had lunch," says Jonathan. "He was doing well, five kids, pleasant wife. He gave me something."

I did not see what happened. I learned about it from Matthew. My call time was ten-thirty, and the accident happened just before ten, so I was still drinking coffee in my tent. I could hear Matthew calling my name, at first from a great distance, then closer and closer, so that I had plenty of time to move. By the time he reached me I was already standing outside with my half-empty mug in my hands.

"Mrs. Raffe, Mrs. Raffe." He was panting, and his shirt was wet with perspiration. He had come a long distance. "Oh, Mrs. Raffe. There has been a terrible accident."

What did I imagine? I do not remember. I said, "Jonathan."

But Matthew shook his head. "No, no. Not Mr. Raffe. He has sent me to find you. He is terribly upset."

"Please," I said. What I meant was *tell me* but Matthew seemed to think that I was offering my coffee, because he took the mug from me and finished it. "Matthew," I said. "What happened?"

"I told them to be careful. They were ahead of me. It was not my fault, Mrs. Raffe. I told them." The mug shook in his slender hands, and I realized for the first time that he was only a boy, probably not even seventeen. I made him come into the tent, and I sat beside him on the cot while he drank a full mug of coffee. Then he told me.

Half of the crew had crossed to the north side of the river before Jonathan and David, who was carrying the camera himself because we were short-handed. The two were in the middle of the bridge when one of the supporting beams gave way, and the entire structure collapsed sideways toward the upper end of the river. Jonathan managed to cling to the ruin, but David was swept underneath, probably because he'd not yet let go of the camera. From both banks, the crew watched helplessly as he was borne along the heavy current. As soon as Jonathan managed to reach the north bank, he began to run along the water's edge, calling the others to help. The Africans, Matthew told me, wisely stayed where they were. But the British and American crew followed Jonathan's direction, all rushing downstream on both sides of the river, apparently hoping to catch David at the next bend in the river.

"I told them no. I shouted and shouted that they should not run along the river bank. Even Mr. Bromley himself was shouting no. He knew. We tried, Mrs. Raffe, we both tried, but they would not stop."

I stared at him. "But why should they not run along the river bank?" I asked. "I don't understand. Didn't David want them to help him?"

"Mrs. Raffe," he said, "he could have found his way out, perhaps. He did drop the camera. He could have floated nicely to shore, and then he might have had a small chance. The trouble is the crocodiles that rest along the banks where the shadows are cool. If you run near, they go into the water. They are very fast."

I felt suddenly sick.

"Mrs. Raffe," said Matthew. "I am so sorry. I could not stop them. I am so very sorry." And he began to cry with me.

"Did you know," asks Jonathan, "that crocodiles can live to be a century old? That is, if they're not shot for shoes or handbags or folk remedies. It is possible that if it is not being worn on the feet of some Milanese matron, the crocodile that ate David Bromley will live another seventy years or more."

The gnocchi have congealed on my plate. My hands are in my lap. They are clasped as if each one offers salvation to the other. I could tell them that they might as well not bother.

"Crocodiles," says Jonathan, "cannot chew their meat. They drag their prey underwater to drown, and if it is too big to swallow at once, they tuck it away neatly under a rock or a waterlogged bough until it is tenderised by decay. It's rather like hanging game, Gillian. Do you remember those marvellous pheasants we used to buy from that butcher on Westbourne Grove? The irony is that I learned all of this from David himself, not two days before his accident. He knew just about everything there was to know about crocodiles after making that fascinating documentary with what's his name? That German... But that's getting off-track. The thing is, the Tanzanians got tired of watching their rotten bridges falling into the river and other Tanzanians being eaten by crocodiles, so they decided to build a better bridge with more substantial footings. And while they were excavating the bank, one of the workmen found something tucked beneath a tree root."

"Jonathan." I don't say *don't*. I don't say *please*. He knows I mean to silence him, but he will not be silenced.

"But don't you want to know what it was, Gillian?"

I don't answer.

Jonathan smiles, creating what in a screenplay is called a beat, a small moment encased in parentheses, during which no one speaks. I have the impression that he realizes this. I have the impression that he is telling this story in the same way that he would shape a film. Right now, for instance, he would create a brief cutaway to Matthew, who would be reaching out a hand to touch my shoulder. This hand would be seen from my point of view, for this is my flashback. And now the camera must come back to my face and Jonathan's words must be heard as off-screen dialogue, for neither his expression nor our surroundings are important to the telling of this story. What is important is my reaction. This is what he is waiting for.

"He found David Bromley's wallet. Remarkable, isn't it? Matthew guessed that it must have been wedged in there, inside David's trousers pocket. Then, when the crocodile went back to retrieve his meal, David came out and the wallet stayed put. Anyway, there it was. Matthew had saved it. He had no idea how to get in touch with any of the *Lion Hunt* crew and he was as pleased as punch when I showed up. He seemed to think it was a sort of burden he was carrying. He asked me to return it to David's family. There were some banknotes, family photos, driver's licence, a few other things he'd taken the trouble to dry out and put back again. A little wrinkled and muddy, but all still legible.

"The thing is, I was in a bit of a bind. Tilly was dying. She'd remarried years ago. Joseph Reardon had adopted the three Bromley children, and from what I could tell, until Tilly's illness, they were all happy as clams. I didn't think it would be *de rigueur*, if you know what I mean, to show up at her deathbed with her first husband's wallet. Anyway, I gave the banknotes to Matthew."

He is leaning back, lighting another cigarette, squinting through the smoke. "As for the rest, I thought about it all the way back to London. By the time I reached Heathrow I was beginning to feel as if Matthew's burden had been passed on to me, only now it was ten times heavier. And then I thought, I'll bet there's something here that old Gillian would like to have. Maybe the pictures of those poor, fatherless children. Or, for all I know, maybe she'd like the entire thing. In any case, it will be a weight off my mind to pass it along."

I am just saying, "I don't—" when he reaches into his pocket, brings out the wallet, and slaps it down on my bread and butter plate. It is thin and misshapen and smells vaguely disagreeable.

"There was a moment," he says, "when I suddenly found myself in the water with Bromley. I suppose I must have looked as surprised as he did. Then I saw some other expression in his eyes, something I couldn't at first fathom. I tell you, he could have grabbed onto the bridge, just as I did, only he had his arms around that damned camera. I suppose he was expecting me to help. I started to reach for him, but for some reason, I just couldn't seem to span the distance. And wouldn't you know it, in the heat of the moment, I completely forgot everything he'd told me about the crocodiles on the banks. At the time, all I could think of was to go after him. Rather good of me even to bother trying, I'd say, considering that he'd just slept with my wife. Darling? Are you all right?"

I hear blood rush to my head as I stare at Jonathan. His face is lit with ghastly triumph. I try to speak, but he stops me, wagging a finger under my nose.

"Yes," he says. "It was just like that, his expression. That last look, as he went bobbing down the river, was comprehension."

Hunky
by Hugh Garner

In just sixty-six years, Hugh Garner saw a lot of life. He grew up in Toronto, fatherless and poor. He rode the rails during the Depression. He fought in both the Spanish Civil War and World War II. He lived hard and wrote about people who did the same in the working class areas of Toronto, particularly Cabbagetown, also the title of perhaps his most famous novel. He wrote realistic literary novels, hundreds of short stories and articles, including stories for CBC radio where "Hunky" first aired. His vision is dark, often angry, concerned for the victim. He also pioneered the Canadian police procedural in three novels featuring Inspector Walter McDumont, beginning with *The Sin Sniper* in 1970. In 1963, Hugh Garner won the Governor General's Literary Award.

It was a hot August morning. The sun, still low against the horizon, was a white-hot stove lid that narrowed the eyes and made the sweat run cold along the spine. The sky was as high and blue as heaven, and the shade-giving cumulus wouldn't form until noon. Before us lay the serried rows of tobacco, armpit high and as dull green as bile. Along with Hunky and the other members of the priming gang I sat in the grass at the edge of the Ontario field waiting for the stone-boat to arrive from the farmyard. The noise of the tiny tractor coming down the dusty track from the yard hid the scratching sound of the grasshoppers in the hedge.

Hunky, to give him the name he called himself, was the gang's pace-setter and also my room-mate in the unused tool shed where we bunked. He sat in the grass, effortlessly touching the toes of his sneakers with the palms of his hands, a redundant exercise considering the limbering up we were getting from our work in the fields. Hunky was proud of his physique, and had a bug about physical fitness, and he practised every evening with a set of weights he had put together from an old Ford front axle with the wheels attached. He believed in health and strength as some believe in education. He had said to me on my first evening on the farm, "Me, I'm a poor D.P. No brains, only strong back. Keep strong, always find job." There was enough truth in his philosophy to make me feel a little ashamed of my own softness, but even more ashamed of the education and training I'd thrown away over the years.

When Kurt arrived on the tractor, he pulled the boat with its high boxed sides into the aisle between the fourth and fifth rows of the new field. When he glanced back at us we got to our feet, my protesting muscles and sinews stiff from the twelve hours of disuse that bridged the time between the morning and the evening before. Without a word we walked to our rows and crouched between them, tearing off the sand leaves like destructive ants, and cradling them in the crook of our other arm. We shuffled ahead on our haunches through a world suddenly turned to jungle, along a sandy aisle that promised an ephemeral salvation at the other end of the field.

Hunky was soon several yards ahead of me, his gilded shoulders bobbing and weaving two rows away, his crewcut nodding up and down between the plants. When he crossed my aisle on his way to the stoneboat he would give me an encouraging wink. The pride he felt in his speed and skill was apparent in his stride and in the way he flaunted his wide armful of green and yellowing leaves before the straw boss, Kurt. At the opposite side of the tractor, McKinnon, Frenchy Coté and Old Man Crumlin were farther back than Hunky and me. Kurt fidgeted on the tractor seat, trying to hurry them with angry glances when he caught their eye.

When I reached the end of my rows Hunky was stretched out in the shade of the tobacco, his head resting in the sand. With an indolent finger he was tracing the rivulets of sweat that ran along his throat. When he saw me he sat up.

"You do good for new man, George," he said.

"Yeah," I answered, throwing myself on the grass.

"You come to farm too late this summer. Better to be here for suckerin'. Taking suckers first make it better to prime after. Loose up muscles," he said. He stretched out an arm that showed the mice running under the chocolate tan of his skin.

"I think you're right, Hunky."

"How many years are you George?"

"Forty-five at the last count."

He shook his head solemnly. "Priming is young man's job. How you get job with Vandervelde?"

"The usual way. From the slave market in Simcoe."

"Why you take job on tobacco, George?"

I didn't want to go into that. My domestic and financial fall from grace would have taken all morning to tell. "I needed the money."

"Yes," he said soberly. Then he brightened up. "How old is Hunky, George?"

I pushed myself up on an elbow and looked him over. "I'd say twenty-four, twenty-five."

"Twenty-t'ree, George. Born nineteen and t'irty-five." Then proudly, "I got papers."

I smiled and lay down again. I thought of the rows upon rows still to be primed of sand leaves, the lowest leaves on the plant. After the sand leaves were gone the work would become easier, as we harvested the leaves higher and higher on the stalk. It was a promise that kept me going almost as much as my desperate need of the money.

"Time to go, George," Hunky said, getting up.

I stood up as Kurt disengaged the tractor from the loaded stoneboat, hitched on to an empty one that had been waiting at the end of the field, and pulled it into an aisle midway between the next ten rows. He waited impatiently until the five of us began working again, then rehitched the tractor to the loaded boat and drove back towards the yard, where the leaf-handlers and tyers were waiting.

Hunky was right; priming tobacco is a young man's job. This was my third day at the Vandervelde farm, and I was surprised I had lasted so long. The beginning of each day was a torture that became an aching hell by evening. Fifteen years of losing jobs on newspapers is no training for manual labour. Though I was sweating heavily, I could no longer smell the exuded alcohol, which was something I was glad of.

At noon hour Mrs. Vandervelde banged the stick around the brakedrum to call us to dinner, and we stumbled up the dusty road, following the tractor and stoneboat to the house. Hunky ran ahead as he always did, to shower under the crude pipe that was rigged behind the kilns. As I passed I could see him behind the gunny sack curtains, his face raised into the guttering stream of water. I just washed my hands.

The table was set out in the yard, under the shade of an oak tree. The two male tyers, and the women leaf-handlers, Frenchy Coté's wife and another French-Canadian girl, were already eating. I don't know too much about Belgian cooking, but the Vandervelde farm was not the place to make a study of it. We had boiled beef again for the third straight day, with boiled turnips and potatoes. Marie Vandervelde, the eighteen-year-old daughter of the farmer, strained against her dress as she ladled food onto our plates. We swallowed it as fast as we could, before the flies could beat us to it.

Hunky came to the table in a minute or two, the water running out of his hair and forming glycerine drops on his shoulders. Marie rubbed against him as she filled his plate. He gave her a shy smile, then disregarded the flies as he bowed his head and crossed himself before he ate. There were plates of doughnuts under cheesecloth covers, but I settled for a mug of coffee. My admiration for Hunky was slightly soured with envy. I wished I'd had a son like him, if I'd had a son. I couldn't even remember ever being as young and healthy myself.

The Vanderveldes, the North Carolina tobacco curer called Joe, and Kurt Gruenther, all ate in the kitchen; the rest of us ate in the yard unless it was raining. As we sipped our second coffee, smoked, and talked together in either English or French, Maurice Vandervelde came through the kitchen doorway and walked down the slope of the yard to the table.

"Kurt tells me you're not getting all the sand leaves," he said.

All the primers but Hunky looked up at him.

"From now on I want every leaf primed," he said, standing there with his hands on his hips like a fat Belgian burgomaster. "Crumlin, and you too Taylor," he said, looking at me. "I want every leaf. You can go over the rows again after supper. I want them plants stripped."

"No leafs left on plants," Hunky said, fixing the boss with his eye. He took an insolent bite of doughnut and washed it down with coffee.

Vandervelde stared down at him, while two white spots appeared on his cheeks. He said, "I didn't say nothing about *your* rows."

Hunky asked, "Why Kurt not say nothing in the field?"

They remained facing each other for a long minute, held apart by something more than fear or respect. "Don't forget what I told you," Maurice said, then swung around on his heel and walked back to the house.

Before we started priming in the afternoon, Hunky walked to the tractor and had a long argument in German with Kurt. Kurt got down from the machine and followed Hunky along the rows we'd primed that morning. When they came back, Hunky was carrying ten or twelve limp yellow leaves. He threw them into the boat with an angry gesture, before disappearing into the tobacco and beginning work.

Nothing was said about the priming at supper, and Maurice stayed in the house. The men each took a shower behind the kilns and the two French-Canadian girls were allowed to use the bath in the house because it was Saturday night. After my shower I put my shorts and extra shirt to soak in a pail. Then I lay on my bunk with the shed door open, watching Hunky lifting his weights in the yard. I heard the laughing chatter of the two girls as they got into Frenchy's car, then watched it pull down the road in the direction of Simcoe with Frenchy at the wheel.

Hunky showered and shaved, then took his white shirt and beige-colored slacks from the hanger beneath his jacket.

"You stayin' here, George?" he asked.

"Yeah, Hunky. I think I'll stay away from town for a while."

"You want a couple of dollars, George?" he asked. "I go now to get my money up at house."

"No thanks. I've got enough for tobacco and papers for next week. That's all I need."

"Hokay. See you Monday morning. You feel good by Monday, you see, George." He laughed.

"I want to thank you for what you did today. If it hadn't been for you, Crumlin and I would have had to go over our rows tonight."

"Was nothing, George. Gruenther try to make trouble, is all. He not make trouble for Hunky though. No siree, not for Hunky." We both laughed at the preposterous thought.

"Are you going away for the weekend?" I asked.

"Sure t'ing. Go to Delhi. Stay with Polish family. Go to church." He pulled a small book from his pocket and showed it to me. The printing was in Polish, but it was half-filled with columns of figures and weekly dates. Most of the figures were for small amounts of money, and showed a total of $350. "Polish people credit union," he explained. "After save for couple years, buy tobacco farm. Tonight I put in fifty dollar, make four hundred, eh, George?"

"You're a rich man, Hunky."

"No important, George. More better to be healthy, eh?" He laughed, slapped me on the shoulder, and left the shed. I watched him take his old bicycle from the barn and wheel it to the house. He disappeared inside for a few minutes, then came out and rode away in the direction of Delhi.

The slight evening breeze dropped with the setting of the sun. McKinnon and Crumlin who bunked in the barn, dropped by to ask me if I wanted anything from the crossroads store about a mile down the road. I gave McKinnon enough money to get me a package of makings, but turned down their invitation to accompany them.

After a while I gave up trying to feel sorry for myself, and thinking how stupid I'd been to end up this way, priming tobacco. I got up and walked across the yard. In the dark the farm had the shadowed realism of a stage set, the big frame house with its windbreak of poplars, the oak tree dominating the yard, the barn, and greenhouse and, behind them, the five tall kilns. Numbers 1, 2 and 3 were belching oily smoke from their chimneys as the tobacco slowly cured.

As I circled the house, listening to the cicadas in the poplars and the cadenced beep of a predatory nighthawk somewhere in the darkening sky above, I heard Maurice shouting inside the house. I was too far away to hear the words, or even understand the language, but I could see the fat form of the boss through the living-room window, pointing a finger at Marie and shouting. Kurt was standing against the door wearing a self-satisfied smirk. Mrs. Vandervelde was remonstrating with her husband, and holding him by the arm. I knew they were discussing Hunky. I turned around and walked towards the kilns.

Joe the curer was sitting in a tilted chair propped against No. 4 kiln, listening to a hill-billy program on his portable radio. He was mumbling to himself and keeping time with his feet. He nodded to me but said nothing. In a moment or two Kurt Gruenther came from the direction of the house, said hello to Joe but not to me, and bent over and peered into the fire-box of No. 3. He spent most of his evenings around the kilns, ambitious to become a curer himself. I went back to the tool shed.

It was some time later when I heard the screen door bang at the house. I looked through the doorway of the shed and saw young Marie come out on the porch and stand there crying. She was soon joined by Kurt, and the two of them sat together on the porch steps. Once, I heard her giggle, and I knew that her tears when her father had been shouting at her had been protective ones.

She wasn't the girl Hunky should think of marrying, but who was I to think of anything like that? What she did when Hunky was away was her own business. I'd woke up a couple of times in the late evening and found Hunky missing from his bunk, and once I'd seen him returning from the fields with Marie. I mused on the thought that the affairs of the young are the envies of the middle-aged. I got undressed and climbed beneath the blanket.

During the next week we finished the sand leaves, and began priming higher up on the plants. Almost imperceptibly the pain and stiffness of the first few days disappeared. I found myself even looking forward to the meals, which showed me my physical cure was almost complete. Sometimes I went most of the day without even thinking of a drink.

The weather held good for priming. There was a heavy dew in the morning, which evaporated shortly after we reached the fields. All the day the scorching sun burned down on the tobacco, tinting the sea-green leaves with lighter hues, yellowing their edges and bringing them to ripeness. Midway during the morning and afternoon Marie came out to the field, carrying a pail of barley water and a dipper, which she set down at the end of the rows. Kurt always stepped down from the tractor to talk to her and take the first drink. The girl laughed a little too loudly at his jokes, her eye roving down the aisle where Hunky was working. After she had stretched her stay as long as she could she would walk back towards the house, her step a little less hurried than when she came.

In the early evenings Hunky and I generally sat on the steps of the shed and talked. He told me about his childhood, which wasn't a childhood at all, but had been spent on a German farm during the war. I knew from hints he dropped that his parents had been put to death in the gas chambers of a

German concentration camp. From things he told me I came to realize that physical fitness and strength were not youthful fads with him, but were the legacy of a time when to be weak or ill meant death.

His ambitions were the modest ones of most immigrants: to buy a place of his own, marry, and have children. He placed great stress on the fact that he hoped to become a Canadian citizen in the fall. His longing for citizenship was not only gratitude and patriotism towards the country that had given him asylum, but a craving for status as a recognized human being.

He seemed very thoughtful one evening, and finally he said, "I never know the good life, George."

"Some of us never do, Hunky."

"After October things change though, eh? I have Canadian passport then, eh, George."

"Sure, you'll be okay then."

"I never before have passport. Never."

He reached into the inside pocket of his jacket hanging on the wall and pulled out a piece of folded paper, its folds blackened from constant opening and its outside surfaces yellowed with age and exposure. It was an immigration clearance from a displaced persons camp near Martfeld, Lower Saxony. Now I remembered his pride when he had told me, a week before, that he had papers. This flimsy thing was Hunky's only proof that his life had a beginning as well as a present. It was all that connected this big, quiet, honest, muscular human being with the rest of documented humanity. I read his name, Stanislaw Szymaniewski, and beneath it his birthplace. Piotrikōw, Poland. Beside the printed question, "Date of birth" was typed July 24, 1935.

"My name is hard for Canadian to say, eh?" Hunky asked. "Hunky not so hard, eh, George?"

I suddenly realized that Hunky is a good name, depending on how it is said. It made me smile a little bitterly to myself to think how he had acquired it. It had probably been some native-born jerk in a railroad bunk-car or construction boarding-house somewhere who had named him that. Whoever he was, he must have been abashed when Hunky adopted the sarcastic epithet as his own.

The harvest was going well, but there was a tension in the air. Vandervelde came out to the fields more and more as the days passed. He would stand beside the tractor and talk to Kurt, while the little German's eyes would stare at us balefully from his small, dark, pinched face, trying to hurry us with an unspoken threat. One quarter of the barn floor was piled high with the cured tobacco, and the five kilns throbbed with the heat from their flues day and night as the leaves dried and cured.

"What's the matter with Vandervelde?" I asked Hunky one night.

"He's scared. Plant too big crop. He owe big mortgage on farm. Have to borrow money from Gruenther for seed last spring."

"From Kurt?"

"Sure. Kurt want Marie, so lend father money. Maurice give him share of crop. Now both scared." He laughed.

"Hunky."

"Yeah, George?"

"Do you like Marie a lot?"

"Sure. She good strong girl, like girl in old country. She—"

"Has she said she'll marry you?" I blurted out.

He stared at me, and there was a hint of sorrow in his sudden anger.

"You think I not good enough for her, George?"

"I didn't say that," I said, turning away.

"We go to dances in the spring, or a movie-picture in Simcoe. Why you ask that, George?"

"Nothing. I've noticed she likes you better than Kurt."

"Sure," he said, smiling again with youthful assurance. "Her father not like me, though."

"I can see that, too."

"He try to make Marie stop meeting me," he said, laughing once again.

I looked at Hunky and wanted to tell him what I thought, but I couldn't. I hoped he never would marry Marie, but for opposite reasons than her father's. He was too good for her, too naïve and unspoilt to let a girl like that break him down. She wore her dresses too tight, and cut her hair too short, and laughed too easily to ever settle down as the wife of an immigrant farmer. Some day she would take off for the city with a good-looking harvest hand, or run away with a salesman of waterless cookers. She was too ripe to stay on the tree but not quite ripe enough yet to go bad. Hunky deserved a better deal from a life that up to then had dealt him only deuces. He was so sure, so youthfully sure, that his health and strength would get him out of any situation. How could I warn him that life wasn't that uncomplicated, that youth and strength were no match for a young woman's wiles and an older man's hatred? He would have to learn it himself, as we have all had to learn at one time or another.

"Maurice want Marie to marry Kurt," he said. "I got no money. I'm only poor Polish D.P."

"But Vandervelde and Gruenther are immigrants too."

"Sure, but got citizenship."

My thoughts about the girl, and his constant harping about passports, "papers," and becoming a citizen, made me angry. He seemed to think that once he received his papers he would no longer be an unschooled labourer: that in some magic way it would make him the equal of anyone in the country.

"Citizenship! I'm a citizen and what has it got me! You'd think it was the most important thing in the world!" I shouted.

He said quietly, "When you have none, George, it is most important thing."

When I cooled down I asked, "Where are you going after the harvest?"

"I got job in Beachville—in limestone quarry. Polish friend work there."

"Are you thinking of taking Marie with you?"

He laughed and slapped his thigh. "Sure t'ing, George! What Maurice say to dat, eh?"

I had a pretty good idea.

Hunky walked to the side of the shed and picked up his homemade bar bells. From my seat on the steps I saw Marie standing on the porch watching him, straining forward in her dress as he was straining as he hefted the bar. It was like watching a piece of taut elastic that is about to break. I went inside again and rolled a cigarette.

The following evening as we hung tobacco in No. 2 kiln, old man Crumlin reached too far for a lath of tobacco and fell from the peak to the earthen floor, breaking his wrist on the way down on a horizontal two-by-four. Maurice Vandervelde ranted and cursed, almost accusing Crumlin of falling just to spite him. He claimed he didn't have enough gas in his car to drive him to the hospital in Simcoe, and Frenchy Coté had to take him in his. The rest of us worked until dark, filling the kiln, though Hunky did the work of two men.

It was getting late in the season, and help was scarce. From then on there were only four of us in the priming crew, and Kurt refused to get down off the tractor to give us a hand. Despite Kurt's weasel glances and Vandervelde's curses, Hunky refused to increase the pace.

"We not run along rows, Maurice," he said to the boss one day. "Want tobacco in, get more men."

Vandervelde spat out something in Flemish, turned around and walked from the field. It was only the shortage of help that prevented him from firing Hunky on the spot. From then on we had to fill an extra boat each day, and the sun was setting by the time we'd hung a kiln in the evening.

One noon hour as we sat at the dinner-table, Vandervelde came into the yard with a junk dealer, and pointed to a pile of old irrigation pipe and worn-out appliances near the barn. The dealer backed his truck through the gate, and looked towards the table for some help in loading it.

The boss cried, "Hey, some of you give this man a hand with this stuff."

McKinnon and one of the tyers rose to their feet, but Hunky shouted, "We get paid for work in fields, not load junk." The two men sat down again.

I had been trying to think of whom Hunky reminded me, and now it came to me. It was an old Scots sydicalist I'd met on a road gang in B.C. in the early years of the depression. He had been a Wobbly, with the guts and dignity of his convictions, long before the trade unions and bargaining tables made his kind an anachronism. "Direct action is all the bosses understand," he used to say.

Vandervelde glared at Hunky, before his face cracked with a mean little smile. He called Kurt from the house, and the two of them helped the junkman load his truck. Then the boss walked to the side of the tool shed and picked up Hunky's bar bells. He carried them to the truck and threw them in. "You can have these for nothing," he said to the man, while Kurt laughed at the joke. I glanced at Hunky. He was eating a piece of pie with studied unconcern, but his face was white beneath his tan.

By Saturday there were only a few days priming left, and one half of the barn was piled high with the cured tobacco. Instead of being cheered by this, Vandervelde became more nervous and irritable than ever. He had caught McKinnon smoking in the barn, and with much cursing had moved him in with the two tyers, who slept in a lean-to against the farm house. Once, he spied Marie talking to Hunky at supper, and called her to the house. As she passed him in the doorway he slapped her across the head.

The weather had been too good to last, and there was electricity in the air. Joe's radio reported a low pressure area moving northeast from the Mississippi Valley, through Illinois, Indiana, and Michigan, and expected in Ontario by early evening. The front was accompanied by heavy thunderstorms and a chance of hail.

Hunky lay on his bunk, stripped to his shorts. He had been unusually quiet since talking to Marie as we came in from the field. Suddenly he said, "Maurice gone to Delhi to try borrow money from Grower's Association. Got no cash or insurance, only tobacco in barn."

"How do you know?"

"Marie tell me," he said. "Not get pay tonight."

"We'll get it tomorrow."

"No, George. Have to wait till tobacco is bought. By then is too long for us to wait." He began pacing up and down the floor of the shed. "I know Vandervelde. He's fat pig. Not want to pay us wages."

"What can we do?"

"I find out if he got money in Delhi tonight," he said.

After he dressed he rode off into the quick gathering darkness in the direction of Delhi. Down in the southwest sky the lightning was flashing pink along the horizon. A strange stillness, broken only by the accelerated chirp of the crickets, fell on everything around.

The storm struck about an hour later, sucking the wind from the east at first, then gusting heavy sheets of rain from the west against the side of the shed. The lightning, white and sulphurous now, flashed through every crack in the walls, and the thunder banged sharply overhead before rolling off into the sky. As quickly as it had come, the storm died off to the east, leaving a residue of gently spattering rain and a breeze that was as clean and cool as new-washed sheets. Before the rain stopped I heard Vandervelde's car being driven into the yard. The barn door was unlocked, and the car driven inside. Then the door was locked again.

On Sunday, as those of us who had stayed at the farm were eating dinner, a provincial police car pulled up at the gate and two policemen walked up to the house. They talked with Maurice for several minutes at the door, then walked to their car. Joe the curer told me during the afternoon that Hunky had been killed the night before on the road by a hit-and-run motorist. The police had been checking to find if he had worked at Vandervelde's.

Hunky dead! It didn't seem possible, unless God had played a senseless joke upon the world. Why would it have to be Hunky, riding along on his bike during the storm of the night before, who had to die? Hunky, the Polack kid with the overwhelming desire to become a Canadian. Hunky, who had had enough pain and sorrow already to do the rest of us a lifetime. Hunky, who crossed himself at meals and went to mass. Boy, that was some heavenly joke all right!

At suppertime the others began to jabber about what a good boy Hunky had been, and Frenchy Coté's wife began to sniffle. I left the table, not wanting to talk to them about Hunky, or listen to their indifferent eulogies. Harvest hands are like hoboes, their friendships as casual as the mating of a pair of flies.

The next evening after work I asked Maurice if he'd drive me to Delhi.

"I'm not going to Delhi," he said. "What do *you* want to go there for?"

"To see a friend," I said.

"Who, Stan the Polack?" he asked, laughing his fat ugly laugh.

Though I knew he could kill me with one hand I suddenly wanted to smash his face. I wanted a miracle that would allow me to reach up and pull his face down to where my boots could crush it. I turned away from him with a hatred for my size, and a frustration I hadn't felt for years.

"My car has a flat tire," Vandervelde shouted after me as I walked away. I pretended not to have heard him.

After supper I walked to the back of the barn and peered through a crack in the boards. The boss's car was parked in the middle of the floor, beside the roof-high pile of yellow cured tobacco. There was no sign of a flat tire, but its left front fender was loose and its left headlight broken, as if it had struck something coming from the opposite direction along the road.

Hunky's jacket was still hanging in a corner of the shed. I reached into the inside pocket and pulled out his D.P. Camp release. I thought how proud he had been of his "papers," and I shoved it into my own pocket, determined not to leave it for strangers to find. I knew that Hunky's friends, and the Polish credit union officials in Delhi would look after the funeral. If I couldn't get there to see him for the last time, I'd go to Simcoe and try to forget him.

Frenchy Coté was driving Joe the curer into Simcoe for an evening off, and I bummed a ride into town with him. Kurt was taking care of the kilns.

My evening in town was a failure. I tried a couple of beer parlors, but couldn't stand the noise and laughter. The more I tried to forget my friend the more I thought of him. I was sure Hunky had been right when he said we'd have to wait weeks for our pay. I thought of laying charges against Vandervelde, but changed my mind. Who would listen to a harvest stiff in the middle of the tobacco country? I'd end up on the wrong side of a vag charge myself.

I went to a bootlegger's and bought two bottles of cheap wine, one of which I drank there. I kept remembering Hunky's remark, "I never know the good life, George." It was the tortured cry of the whole bottom half of humanity.

I walked out to the highway with my bottle, and flagged down a car, driven by a young fellow going to St. Thomas. He let me out where the road to the farm led north across the fields towards Vandervelde's. I had some brave drunken idea that I would stand up to the boss and tell him what I knew, then laugh at him as he had laughed at Hunky.

I cut across the fields and had almost reached the farmyard when I saw Marie coming down the path. I hid myself in the hedge, and saw Kurt cutting across towards her from the kilns. When he joined her they went towards the fields, her arm around his waist. They were all rotten, and just accusing Maurice was not enough. I had to hurt them all, for Hunky's sake.

A half hour later I returned to the junction of the side road and the highway and waited for Frenchy to come along. When he did, I flagged him down. I told Frenchy and Joe that I'd been given a lift that far by a young man driving to St. Thomas.

We had almost reached the farm before we met Kurt, running down the road and glancing back every now and then across his shoulder. It was then that we first saw the pillar of whitened smoke hanging over the farmyard.

We pulled up in the yard alongside the fire truck from a small village to the north of us. The barn and two kilns were gutted, nothing remaining but a portion of the barn floor, a few charcoaled posts, and the still-steaming frame of Vandervelde's automobile. Joe jumped out of Frenchy's car and looked at the fireboxes of the other three kilns; the oil feedcocks on all of them had been turned on full, and the tobacco ruined.

The fire chief was telling Maurice that the fire had jumped from the kilns to the barn. Nobody told him any different, although I knew that the breeze was coming from the opposite direction.

Mrs. Vandervelde and Marie stood in the kitchen doorway, alternately sobbing and staring fearfully at Maurice, who now stood in the middle of the yard, not laughing now, but opening and shutting his fat mouth like a landed carp.

The next morning before anyone else was up I walked between the rear of the gutted barn and the cracked and broken greenhouse. On the ground was a half-burned piece of document paper. By bending close I could read the beginning of a name typed along a dotted line: Stanislaw Szym...I crushed it into the mud with my foot. In a way you could call it Hunky's epitaph. But even that didn't seem enough. Not by a goddamn long shot!

Man on the Roof
by Jas. R. Petrin

Over the past twenty years, Jas. R. Petrin has carved out a place as one of Canada's leading writers of short crime fiction. He is proof that people from Winnipeg understand greater social ills than biting mosquitoes and biting cold. Most frequently published in *Alfred Hitchcock Mystery Magazine*, Jim explores the dark undersides of both rural and urban society. Jim has been a multiple Arthur Ellis Award finalist, winning the award in 1989 for his story "Killer in the House." His stories have been anthologized often and adapted for television.

Climbing was no different than any other risky job. You had to be alert. You had to keep your nerve. It had nothing to do with bravado. It was simply a matter of skill. Gorman had climbed hundreds of buildings in his time; this one was no different and that was what he wanted to keep firmly fixed in his mind—the idea that this was routine work.

The fog was good. It would be his friend. It would hide him as he climbed. And more important, since his vertigo attack of three years ago at the Hotel George, its blanketing haze would preserve him from any chance glimpse of the drop below.

The abyss.

The void.

He had scaled the first security fence almost as if it had not been there at all. Up and over. Eighteen feet of barb-topped chain-link and it hadn't even slowed him down. He allowed himself to draw a small pride from that; it was always best in the face of doubt to dwell on one's successes.

He didn't know why the vertigo attack had hit him when it did. Perhaps because he had stayed at the work too long. All he knew was that in a single moment he had gone from a confident, practised professional climbing smoothly up the wall of the Hotel George, one hundred feet above the street, to a man stricken with a terror so paralyzing it had reduced him to a trembling coward in a single instant. The vertigo had seized him like a taloned hawk. It was as if the city, one moment spread out below him in lethargic neon majesty, had lurched suddenly into motion, proceeding grandly in a huge, slow revolution around him as his blood clotted in his veins, his mouth dried, his heart hammered at his ribs like a captive wanting out. His fingers embedded themselves like hooks into the fissures of the mortar and brick. Mind and body in mutiny against him.

Dawn came. Morning passed. Still he clung there. Pigeons fluttered and cooed curiously around him. It was 10 a.m. before he was spotted and the police and fire department crawled in below like Matchbox toys to fetch him down; he rode to the police station in the back of a patrol car in handcuffs, trembling uncontrollably, like a man with fever.

It was not being in custody that caused him to shake; it was dealing with the fact that he had lost his nerve. He had never once even considered the possibility that it could happen to him, and he *had* lost his nerve.

He had sworn he would never climb again. More important, three years later he had sworn he would never climb for LaCoste.

But here he was.

Gorman crossed the grassy strip of ground that separated the fence from the outer wall, moving quickly but carefully in the fog. He kept his eyes open for trip wires. This was no fat and sleepy hotel where room guests sprawled half-drunk in their beds with their jewelry lying out on their bedside tables next to their pocket change. He was dealing with professionals here, the best in the business. It would pay to remember that.

At the wall of the building he stopped, stood inches away from it for a moment, hands spread wide and pressed up flat against the stone. He was like an artisan measuring his work. The wall was gritty and chill, damp with the mist that had stolen down along the river from the marshes in the north.

There was almost no wind. That was good too. He took the light aluminum grapnel from his belt, hefted it on its thin rope, whirled it until it whickered and then let it fly. It tinkled over the parapet high above and held, first time. An omen. A sign that there was nothing to fear, that he had not lost his touch. His hands gripped the thin Dacron line, snapped it taut, then took up its elasticity gently with the weight of his body as he began to walk the wall.

He could do this one last job. He knew he could. Even though it should never have come to this, an old man back at a young man's game. He had assets put by; he could have retired after doing his time. That was one reason why he had turned down the work offered to him by LaCoste in the first place.

He had not liked his new cellmate, LaCoste, who was a quick little man, defiant and shrewd. He looked like a snitch, smelled of dried sweat and he spent too much time in lockdown to be completely trusted: a younger man letting on he was oh-so-well-schooled in crime but who was too untried, too laughably inexperienced to be convincing. And he'd been wheedling. He wanted Gorman's help.

"Lori's smart," he had said. "She never steers me wrong about the take. There was a fortune in that place, in spite of what happened. Believe it." His girl was a cleaner with a maid service. She was also very good at opening locks. It was a fine scam she and LaCoste had got going. Being bonded and an obvious suspect, she never took anything herself but simply spotted for LaCoste, took inventory, sketched maps, prepared the way. It was simple enough to leave a door or a casement latch ajar—he had heard LaCoste joke that she was one of the few cleaning ladies who still did windows.

Gorman was annoyed. "So why are you telling me?"

LaCoste sat on the edge of his lower bunk blinking up at him, nose twitching. He looked startlingly like an oversized rodent, sharp-featured and supple. His hair was pulled back from his brow, slick as an oiled pelt. Even his skin glistened. He looked as though, with a minimum of effort, he could press himself through the bars, oil his way through the many doors and gates and escape back into the sewer from which he had come.

"Why am I telling you?" he repeated. "Why am I telling you? Because you're the best, that's why. Everybody knows that." Had LaCoste not heard of Gorman's vertigo attack at the top of the Hotel George? Apparently not. Except for a few policemen, Gorman was sure that nobody knew—only his own soulmate, Mila. "You climb like a cat," LaCoste said. "That's the word. You could break into the top floor offices of the Trizec without passing through the lobby or cracking a window—you'd run up the outside walls and get in down the chimney. I need a man like that for high-wire jobs. Eagle's nests. I need an expert. There's nobody else comes close. And you're available."

Gorman lay on his top bunk, hands behind his head, wishing the little rat would shut up. "You're sure of that, are you?"

"Course I'm sure. Why shouldn't I be? I heard the guards talking. You're out of here, back on the street at the end of the month. What is it? Two, three weeks?"

Gorman had spent the better part of three years on the inside; LaCoste had arrived to begin his stay only a few weeks ago, after his last job had gone wrong.

"In seventeen days, eleven hours and..." Gorman consulted his watch "...twenty-three minutes—I'm out of here."

The rodent leered. He had yellowish, wide, sloping teeth that could have gnawed through a leg-iron. "You sound anxious."

"Everybody in here is anxious. But I can wait. If I wanted to I could walk out of here tonight." It was a childish boast and he regretted making it before the words were out of his mouth. But it was true. He had the route worked out, and the method. In three years of confinement he had learned which guards could be bribed to look the other way, to leave a latch undone. The rest would be easy for a high-wire man. A quick climb to the roof through the air conditioning ducts and from there across the tiles, away from the main block to a less secure, less well-lighted wing and then down. Piece of cake for a high-wire man.

Only for this high-wire man, the thought of those heights made his head reel.

"So why don't you go then? What are you waiting for?"

Because I'm afraid I might fall, he almost said. Instead he replied, "I'm almost a free man. Why take the risk?"

The rodent studied him. "You'll be wanting work when you get out. You'll be wanting some cash." LaCoste didn't know about Gorman's retirement fund either; there was a lot LaCoste didn't know. He was an abysmally ignorant little man. "You'll be wanting something to sharpen your claws on, some quick jobs where you can pick yourself up a little operating capital. I got those jobs and all the background information you need to bring them off. I'm a climber. I'd do them all myself if I could, but I'm locked in here. Lori would work with you if I told her to." He laughed. "It might be a great set-up for me, I'd be safe in here, wouldn't I? But I need you, Gorman. We can cut a deal. Something more than fair, seeing as I'd do all the prep work."

"But I'd do all the climbing, would I?"

The rodent shrugged; his shoulders were so narrow they seemed hardly to go up and down. "What can I tell you? You're the high-wire man, aren't you? You're the expert—like a plumber. When a pipe needs fixing you don't go at it with Scotch tape and string, you call in a plumber. I trust experts to do their thing."

"I'm going to retire."

"You got lots of years left. We'd be partners."

"You screwed up on your last job."

The rodent's lip curled. "You read about it?"

"I don't read the papers. They depress me."

"Well, I don't mind telling you, Gorman, I get rattled when I climb. My nerves… And then, if something goes wrong inside…" He let out a long whistling breath. "If something goes wrong inside, like there's somebody at home, or something, I tend to get excited, know what I mean? I tend to get rough. Now, in that last job…"

Gorman was curious. He rolled on his side and looked down over the edge of the bunk.

"What about that last job?"

Pleased at Gorman's interest, LaCoste sat up. His little eyes jerked about as he recalled the scene. His speech grew more animated.

"A mistake. Just a mistake. Lori did her best, but... It's why I'm here. I knew the schedule of the place. There wasn't supposed to be anyone home. It was supposed to be empty, the woman out visiting, the old man away like he'd been for ages, God knows where. Only, there she was anyway."

"There was who?"

"The woman. Who else? It's funny. I was so sure I was alone in that place, I was standing in the den taking a cozy look around, then in she walks straight out of the kitchen at me. I must've jumped as high as she did. Then...I guess maybe I panicked."

Gorman looked at his cellmate, at the furtive, leaping eyes, the narrow, shiny face and he saw lurking there the violence that the woman must have seen, the explosive ferocity of a small cornered animal. Disgusted, he lay back down on his bunk and looked at the ceiling again. He despised amateurs.

"So you assaulted her," he said.

"Well, what was I supposed to do? Sit down and watch while she phoned the cops on me? What would you have done?"

"I sure as hell wouldn't have done that."

"Well," said LaCoste, "that's the whole point, isn't it? I said I needed you, didn't I?"

LaCoste was talking fast as he always did, but there was an ill-concealed resentment beginning to smolder behind his little liquid eyes, pique at Gorman's reluctance, at Gorman's obvious contempt. His pupils moved in quick short leaps tracking Gorman's own: left, right, then back again. "So Lori screwed up. Everybody's allowed one screw-up, ain't they?" He reached up from his lower bunk to grip Gorman's knee, a gesture of solidarity, but Gorman's skin crawled. "Come in with me. Hell of a deal, pal. You can't say no."

Gorman peered down into the clever little eyes with distaste and wondered what LaCoste would do if he were to reach down and yank out those ridiculous scraggly hairs that the silly ass called a beard.

Gorman gained the parapet easily. He stooped to haul in the rope, but did not disturb the grapnel. Force of habit; normally he would need that on his way back. He left the rope coiled neatly beside it and turned to assess the next stage of the climb. There had been less of an effort made here to deny a hand- or foothold; the builders had placed their faith in the featureless face of the lower wall, in the security fence and in the door and gate alarms; they had not given the top forty feet of the building the attention it deserved. A mistake on their part. A vertical four-inch conduit was clamped securely to the brick here, the sort that contained electrical cables. To Gorman it was as good as a ladder. No doubt it had been installed years after the wall was built, a breach in security unforeseen by the original planners.

He gave the pipe a tug, found it solid and began to climb. The mist drifted around him, comforting and soft. In a moment he could no longer see the ground. He felt no fear. What was it LaCoste had said he needed? Something to sharpen his claws on? Perhaps the little rat had been right.

Still, he ought not to be here. Retirement: after his attack, that had been his plan—his and Mila's. There had been more than enough put aside for it. And he would have retired according to plan if there'd been anything left of his life worth retiring to.

He had guarded his private life from the authorities, had not told them where he lived: no fixed address is what they had been forced to log against his name. Nor had he phoned Mila from the prison. Not even to tell her he was coming home. He did not want to take the slightest chance that his call might be traced.

That had been the worst shock of his life, coming after the long lonely bus ride from the prison, rolling away from that swine LaCoste, home to Mila through the night. The penthouse apartment dark and deserted—no Mila waiting. His first emotion upon seeing no light in the topmost windows of the high-rise had been disappointment: how could he call it a homecoming without Mila?

A poorly secured clamp suddenly pulled loose and with a tortured creak the conduit swayed a few inches out from the wall.

Gorman caught his breath, halted. He clung to the pipe at the mercy of the fates. He waited for the screech of metal that would signal the start of his plunge. But after a moment the conduit seemed to stabilize. He began slowly to climb again. A concrete nail had pulled free, that was all. Poor craftsmanship. No one took pride in their work nowadays.

"I'm retiring," Gorman had repeated.

"So come out of retirement."

Gorman kept on thinking about LaCoste's botched break-in.

"Just who was this target you so royally screwed up, anyway?" Gorman felt a twinge of curiosity about LaCoste's operation, even though he had no intention of climbing again. "What was it? *Who* was it?"

"What do you mean, who and what? What difference does that make? A mark, a target. Who cares?"

"A good set-up man cares about everything. He does his homework."

LaCoste's dark face turned poisonous.

"I done my homework! I knew everything I needed to. I knew the layout—living room, bedrooms, the whole floor plan. The alarms. I knew what the stuff in there was worth! My Lori knew before I went in—she seen it!" He drew back from Gorman with an injured look. "Don't tell *me* I never done my homework."

They sat in silence for a while, studying one another. LaCoste would have made a lousy card player. His little eyes tumbled with his thoughts. His hatred was displayed on his face like a sign in a window. Finally he said, "I think I know why you're slideslipping me, Gorman. I can see right through you. Retiring—crap! That's not it at all. You're just plain nervous, aren't you? You don't want no more high work. You can't face it. You've lost your nerve. You're scared."

Hearing LaCoste put into words the fears that had hung wraithlike for so long in the dark at the back of his mind had seemed to lend substance to them, make them more real. They crept out into reality to hide in the corners of the cell, behind the toilet, under the bunks, ready to come at him with their knives and hooks when the lights went out. He shuddered. Last night he'd dreamt he had fallen from the top of the CN Tower onto a wrought iron fence. There had been no sensation of falling, only the whistle of the air in his ears, long minutes of the ground rushing up at him with its row of sharpened spears.

LaCoste took a cigarette from his shirt, lit it with a practised snap of a Zippo lighter, blew smoke out of his nose and tipped his head to one side. All the time he didn't take his eyes off Gorman, watched him like a man who has just witnessed a metamorphosis. Busy eyes. Eyes that never kept still in their sockets.

LaCoste said, "Yeah. I pegged you wrong. I see that now. I'll have to get me somebody else. A younger guy. Somebody with guts."

Gorman's backhand had seemed to lash out of its own volition. It caught the smaller man on the side of his oily face, snapped his head back and sent him spinning sideways off his bunk. But LaCoste was quick. Before he even hit the floor he had a shank in his hand. He seemed to have snatched the wicked blade from nowhere, like a conjuror producing a card.

His breath was ragged in his throat. "Do that once more, Gorman, and I'll kill you, so help me, God. Bulldog me again and I'll rip your throat out." He dragged himself like a wounded cur into his bunk. "You're making a big mistake," he said. "We got a good thing going, me and Lori. I'll retire one day with millions and where'll you be?" He had lain hidden for a moment breathing heavily, then he had said, "I'll get you up on a building again. You'll climb for me yet, Gorman."

And as it turned out, LaCoste had been right.

Gorman reached the top of the pipe. There was a wide rain trough here, flimsily attached. He eased himself over it gingerly, not wanting to cause the slightest sound. And then he was on the roof.

It was a roof of slate tile, with a slope of some thirty degrees. He would have to watch his footing here. A single slip and... But he wasn't going to think about that. He began to move forward, his Nikes finding marginal purchase on the tiles as he put each foot down, rubber soles sliding toward the eaves on the fog-slicked tile. One foot ahead of the other, that was how it was done. A huge bulk loomed out of the mist on his left: a cowling, something to do with the air conditioning; below it would be the network of ducts that he sought; they ran everywhere throughout the old building, a virtual freeway to a man who could climb and gain access. At the peak of the roof a wind-torn bit of flashing projected upward and he had to step over it carefully.

As he straddled the building, one foot on either side of the peak, the fog lifted in the distance and he saw the city, like a ten-mile dance of electric light at the foot of the sky and just for a moment he felt the old thrill of satisfaction that climbing had given him once. A sense of power, of being on top of it all while the rest of the world crawled ant-like below.

Then the fog settled in again, snuffing out the sight. He moved on, angling down the pitch of the roof this time and in a few more minutes he came in sight of his objective—the dome that crowned the top of the main building. All access doors to the roof were routinely and carefully checked, but the dome—perhaps because it was thought to be impregnable—was ignored. Just one more tricky bit of climbing would bring Gorman up to it.

Where the two uneven wings of the main building came together there was a flat wall facing him, perhaps twenty feet high. It was featureless, without a handhold. But there was, he knew, a cornice that followed the older wall and adjoined a matching bit of stonework on the new wing, an effort by the builders of the newer extension to preserve architectural purity. It was as good as a sidewalk to Gorman, a causeway round the periphery of the blank gable-end.

He padded down the slope to the edge of the roof and without hesitation stepped over the eaves and onto the cornice. It wasn't much of a sidewalk, only eighteen inches wide. A trick of the wind tugged the fog away at that moment, and for an instant the ground was visible—a thin thread of highway far-off in the distance where tiny cars followed their lights. Without warning vertigo seized him. It took him in the gut, in the big tendons of his legs, making his body so weak and his knees jerk so violently he had to sit down fast on the brink of the eaves. He tried to swallow, found he had no spit in his mouth, tried to swallow again and trembled.

He heard LaCoste's needling voice echoing in his head, "You can't face it. You've lost your nerve. *You're scared.*"

The wall of the main building dropped away vertically and between his knees he caught a glimpse of a stone courtyard far below, a spidery black iron fence or railing, so much like the one in his dream it made his head go around. Then the fog pushed back in, and he couldn't see the ground anymore, only a swelling of the mist a hundred feet below where it was given body by the sodium glow of the security lights in the forecourt. A shudder pierced him, a violent quaking that shook his entire frame. Perhaps it was worse not being able to see the ground. Too easy to believe the drop was even greater than it really was—more than a hundred feet, perhaps five hundred, a thousand feet, a mile....

With his heart pounding fiercely, he drove these ideas off. Gradually he steadied himself. His body still slick with sweat, the night wind blowing cold upon him freshened him. He got up, took a first step and with the fingertips of his left hand trailing along the wall, slowly walked the cornice past the gable-end that had blocked him. Another fifteen steps brought him face on with a tall dormer window that cut upward through the eaves and peaked high above the roof. Its limestone facing stood out eight inches from the facade, broken where the mortar had slipped from between the stones, an easy stepladder to the roof for a strong and limber man with a steady nerve, a man such as he had once been. His pulse still thumped harshly in his breast, but he went up the facing without missing a step.

Next he climbed the seam at which the dormer met the slope of the roof—much steeper than the roof of the lower wing, but he made it to the top. Once there he straddled the dormer like a boy on a fence row and paused to catch his breath.

He did not intend to fall if he could help it. He had done his homework well on this one. He knew the dome was just above him; he had only to climb the steep gradient of roof tile to reach its base. Still, he did not trust himself to look up at it, even though he knew he must in order to orientate himself with the unlocked trap. And if he did not look up at it, he would not see how the final stage of the climb should be done.

Slowly he tilted back his head, gripped the spine of the dormer more firmly and opened his eyes. The sight that immediately filled his eyes took him instantly back to the Hotel George. The same panic squirmed again in his guts, clawing up into the back of his throat. Lit dimly by some scattered lights that shone below and behind him, the dome was a bulbous black mass. The mist had torn open to give him, in one long rent, the sky, and he saw quick grey clouds scudding above and behind the dome, their direction of motion oblique to the lights he had seen moving on the highway below. The two motions combined seemed to lend the entire rooftop a giddy twisting movement and, just as before, he felt that the building had come alive beneath him.

He gritted his teeth.

He must not give way to panic. Not this time. He must think about Mila. What poor Mila had endured was far worse than this. A fall to the courtyard below would be a merciful end by comparison. He forced himself to dredge up the scenes from that night....

Letting himself into their penthouse suite he found its contents tumbled and tossed, disarranged first by the intruders and then, as he learned later, by the police. Fear had struck him as he surveyed the devastation—true fear. Fear for Mila. He had dashed into the bedroom calling for her, found it torn to pieces, a scene of violence. The wall safe behind the head of the bed hung open like a tiny gutted tomb.

Half-crazed he had dragged the building manager out of bed, a nervous little Rumanian who, alarmed at Gorman's state, had babbled almost hysterically to him about the break-in.

"It was months ago. They came from the *outside*, Mr. Gorman. Who would have thought it possible at such a height?"

"*And Mila?*" he had screamed, seizing the manager by his pyjama-front and hoisting him into the air. "What about Mila?"

The manager knew little. Only that the intruder had dealt her a heavy blow to the head. "She must have awakened and surprised him." They had wheeled her out on a gurney and down to a waiting ambulance. There had been much confusion. Policemen in uniforms and plainclothes. Questions, so many questions. But this the manager remembered: Mila had been whisked away to the hospital—perhaps the Misericordia, the one they called the Misery. Perhaps she was still there.

Gorman had driven like a madman through the city. And now, perched at the base of the dome, he recalled her as he had found her there: Mila on the edge of a hospital bed so high her pale blue feet dangled half a foot above the floor. To her, a precipice, higher than any building. Her eyes peaceful, wide, but empty, two round limpid lakes devoid of animation. The delicate hand curling limply in his own; press it—no response. Asking questions and hearing no reply. Gorman had allowed the nursing staff to lead him trembling back to the elevator.

He had spent an hour pacing the dark streets among the tall houses around the hospital, stopping for long minutes to stare out over the river, his anguish for Mila steadily souring into a bitter rage, an emptiness in his gut that was a hunger for vengeance.

But first he must confirm his suspicions. This he could do. Three decades in the life's blood of the crime world gave him an advantage over even the most dedicated police detective. He went back to his car, drove into the core of the city and began his enquiries.

And so what now if he fell?

He opened his eyes again and stared long and hard up at the dome. He saw the thin lines of the maintenance trap etched in dark relief against its tiled skin. The yawning gulf, the abyss inches behind him, was pushed from his mind and he got to his hands and knees. Then he stood. He climbed the steep slope determinedly to the foot of the dome, trod the great rings at its base like steps and started sure-footedly up the curve of the dome itself. As he rose above the protective peak of the roof, the wind suddenly quickened. It rippled his sleeves, snapped his collar at his neck, carried a trailing shirttail streaming behind him like the flag of all crimedom. He was engulfed in a misty turbulence. Like a fly he crawled doggedly up the great inverted bowl of the dome. Fingers and toes; that's all you had. If they failed you, then...

Better to think about Mila!

Think about the guilt—that was the worst.

Without warning the wind fell to nothing, as if it had been called to heel for afflicting the man who climbed like a cat. Gorman inched on up the curving surface. A moment later he was at the trap. If it was locked, if his contacts within had failed him, then his climb had been in vain.

But it was not locked.

The trap lifted easily, as had been arranged; he hoisted it open, climbed a few feet higher, took a last look out over the misted night, then stepped inside, onto the highest trestle of a steel catwalk. He lowered the trap behind him. He would be safe for a while now, able to catch his breath. This was the only place Security did not bother to check on their incessant patrols. It had the added advantage of being handy to the ducts. He needed the ducts. He slipped out the black rubber flashlight he always took with him on a job—black electrical tape encasing it in a tube of thin foam which would deaden its sound should it fall—and switched it on.

The steel catwalk where he perched was one used by maintenance workers who needed access to the roof; it was high above the floor, the uppermost of two levels below the dome. Now he moved quickly, padding down the steel rungs of the catwalk to the landing floor, then down a more substantial staircase to the attic below. There he went purposefully along a dusty corridor, bowing his head to clear the underside of the sloped roof he had scaled a moment ago. At the end, he pushed open a door and found himself in the equipment room which housed the huge metal plenums of the air conditioning ducts. Without hesitation he approached the first of these, unlatched an access panel which hinged outward like a door, clambered inside and shut himself in.

He knew what he must do. He knew the route. He had gone over it for months in his mind. He pressed his head and shoulders into one of the four openings which led from inside the plenum—the second from the left—and stretching out fully on his belly, the flashlight flat out ahead of him, began to worm his way into the duct; the blowers would not come on for at least another hour—that too had been arranged. There was a thick smell of dust that made him want to cough. At one point a vertical shaft opened under his forearms, dropped away into blackness like a well and he had to bridge it with his body and drag himself across. Then a steeply falling slope led him down and down. Fifteen minutes took him to another horizontal passage. Following this, he counted the branchings in the yellow light of the torch, then finally turned sharp right into a horizontal passage. He switched off the torch, writhed forward again as quietly as possible, then came to a stop at a steel grating.

A feeble light glimmered beyond.

He was absolutely sure of his position now.

He took hold of the grating, hooked his fingers into its grid, shifted it gently forward, rotated it slightly, and pulled it inside. The rivets which originally secured it had been filed through months ago when he had been thinking of escape.

The scene below him was familiar. The stairwell at the end of Tier Four. The door that led in to the range itself was off-stop, that too had been managed. He sucked in his breath. He knew the scents. Even the sounds were old acquaintances: the low snores and grunts, the thin brittle coughs reverberating off steel and stone. The heels of the strolling guard ticking distantly somewhere like a clock, the guard who would be nowhere near the quietly unlocked cell where LaCoste now lay in Gorman's old upper bunk, flat on his back the way he always slept, mouth hanging open, eyes shut tight.

LaCoste the mastermind.

The man who did his homework—except that he hadn't even known who he had been robbing.

Gorman eased himself silently out of the duct.

"A Wanton Disregard" copyright 2003 by Jean Rae Baxter.

"A Murder Coming" copyright 1973 by James Powell. Originally published in Ellery Queen Mystery Magazine.

"Bush Fever" copyright 1990 by Peter Sellers. Originally published in *Cold Blood III* as by Jack Paris.

"An Eye for an Eye" copyright 1994 by Nancy Kilpatrick. Originally published in *Cold Blood V*.

"Italics" copyright 2004 by Fabrizio Napoleone.

"Green Ghetto" copyright 2004 by Vern Smith.

"Great Minds" copyright 1999 by Barbara Fradkin. Originally published in *Storyteller Magazine*.

"The Big Trip" copyright 2003 by John Swan.

"Dead Like Dogs" copyright 1985 by William Bankier. Originally published in Ellery Queen Mystery Magazine.

"Crocodile Tears" copyright 2004 by Leslie Watts.

All reasonable efforts were made to secure permissions for "Hunky" written by Hugh Garner.

"Man on the Roof" copyright 1990 by Jas. R. Petrin. Originally published in *Cold Blood III*.